PLAIN AND SIMPLE SERIES®

# Against the Tide

Getting Beyond Ourselves

By
Nancy Missler

**The King's High Way Ministries, Inc.**

KHW

Against the Tide

Copyright 2002 by Nancy Missler

Published by The King's High Way Ministries, Inc.
P.O. Box 3111
Coeur d'Alene, ID 83816
(866) 775-5464
www.kingshighway.org

Third Printing, January 2012

ISBN: 978-0-9745177-0-4

All Scripture quotations are from the King James
Version of the Holy Bible.

PRINTED IN THE UNITED STATES OF
AMERICA

# Table of Contents

# Against the Tide
## Getting Beyond Ourselves

This is a book about *faith*.

This is also a book about *choices*,
because faith <u>is</u> simply a series of choices.

Ultimately, this is a book about having
enough "faith" to "choose" to go *against the
tide*—the tide of our own natural thoughts
and emotions—and follow God.

# Chapter One
## Choices:  The Key to Our Christian Walk

Toni's letter began, "I am married (separated now) to an abusive man who is an on-again-off-again drug abuser.  We have been married now for five years.  In the beginning of our marriage, I prayed for my husband and kept my heart open to God's Love and had such peace.  However, over this past year I have become so bitter as a result of all the betrayals, ugly words and lack of commitment, that I have come to deeply hate this man.

"Today, I just got out of the hospital from losing our child (I was four months along).  I almost lost my life because I hemorrhaged so badly that I was in shock and had to have a blood transfusion.  My husband never even came to see me or call me.

"It's these kinds of things that I seem not to be able to forgive.  When I am in prayer, I truly *want* to be released from all of these negative emotions and to walk in Love, but each time one of these incidents occurs, I react in anger and hatred instead.  It is to the point now where my husband no longer sees his own sin, but instead sees the anger in me.  Thus, he believes he is a good husband and I am the wicked one.

"The question is...*how do I get out of this?  How do I get beyond my emotions when I am so hurt that I can feel it in the deepest part of my stomach?  I just *can't seem to get free from these emotions and I feel like I'm tottering on the edge.*

"I really want a relationship with Jesus again, like it used to be. I pray daily for strength and that I would be able to walk in Love, *but I can't seem to break free from these horrible feelings* that explode when I am confronted with another situation. What do I do? Please help me."

------------------

Bob's letter began, "On October 15th, my wife filed for a legal separation. She placed a restraining order on me and evicted me from our home.

"...the day after being tossed out of my house, I sat in an empty room in a state of shock and said, 'Father, what have I done?' As I wept before the Lord, He began to reveal things that I had never seen before. He showed me that I was all tied up in knots by the enemy and by the indulgences that I had allowed my own flesh to participate in. *I was in the clutches of bitterness, resentment and bound by dependencies that I couldn't even see.* He showed me that while I continually begged Him to make Himself known to my wife, I wouldn't respond to what He was asking me to do. I had chosen to harden my heart against her and had allowed a root of bitterness to grow and grow and grow, until it finally just grew into a mighty tree.

"God showed me that these were the things that caused our problems and this is why He had to 'hit me over the head with a bat' to get my attention. All His previous subtle and gentle attempts had failed.

My cold and hardened heart (full of bitterness and resentment) had simply quenched His Spirit in me.

"But Lord, what do I do now? *How do I get rid of my bitterness and resentment?* And, where do I find the genuine love that I need?"

--------------

Recently, I had a wonderful luncheon with a dear friend. But, towards the end of our time together, Sandy asked my opinion on her personal situation. When I gave her my suggestions, she reacted violently. *"What am I supposed to do, fake it?" She yelled at me. "I simply don't love him anymore. I used to, but I don't any longer! I'm just going to get a divorce!"*

---------------

## "Movers" of our Soul

Natural thoughts, emotions and desires. The dictionary calls them "the movers of our soul," because what we think and feel is what we naturally choose to follow and act upon.

Both Christians and non-Christians alike struggle with these elements of life. Our thoughts stir up our emotions; our emotions influence our desires (or our choices); and our choices produce our lives. In other words, everything we say and do is built upon these driving components of our makeup. Our days are even defined by *how we feel*. We have "good days" and we have bad days. We constantly ask one another, "How do you feel?" "How are you?" Most of the time it's not our physical health that we are inquiring about, it's our mental and emotional status.

What we think and how we feel determines all aspects of our lives, as seen in the comments of the above letters.

Confirming this, listen to some of the book titles and articles that are in our local bookstores and on the internet: *Feel the Fear and Do It Anyway, You Don't Have to Feel This Way, Glamorous Scents for Your Every Mood, Choose Happiness, Intimacy, Feel Good Naked* and *If It Hurts, It Isn't Love.* And, of course, half of the books in the relationship section are on the mental and emotional feelings that go along with sexual intimacy.

If we are not able to control and tame these "movers of our soul," however, they can easily overwhelm and drown us. As someone once dramatically expressed to me: *"I just can't seem to change how I feel. I am a Christian, but I feel how I feel regardless of how much you prove to me that 'I shouldn't feel this way!'"*

Should our thoughts and feelings carry this much weight? Should they be the basis of our choosing, our acting and our existence, especially as Christians? How do we control them? How do we tame them? And, most importantly, how do we get beyond them? As Sandy so aptly stated, "What are we supposed to do, *fake it*?"

The bottom line is, how are we able to go *against the tide* of our own thinking and feeling, choose God's will and still be genuine?

How can Toni break free from her feelings of betrayal by her husband? How can Bob ever get rid of his root of bitterness against his wife? And, poor Sandy, is it possible for her to ever fall in love with her husband again?

These are good questions! And they're questions we all ask. Again, the bottom line is, *how do we change what we really think, feel and want to do, in order to follow God, but still not be phony*? If faith is simply a series of choices to genuinely manifest Christ's Life, what happens when we don't know how to make choices we don't feel?

This is the subject of this book: "How do we, as Christians, overcome the "justified" hurt feelings, the anger, the bitterness, the resentment, the fear, the unforgiveness, the insecurity, the guilt and the memories (the movers and shakers of our soul) that consume us daily? Is it possible to make choices to follow God when we really don't feel like it, want to or even think it will work? Will God honor something we choose simply by faith, but that we don't feel?

## "A Damascus Road Experience"

Here's a remarkable real-life example. Read it and then, you decide.

"It was the last day of our trip home to Florida to visit our family and I was at my husband's parents' house where we'd always stayed, packing alone. All the kids were at the beach and Ken, my husband, was out fishing with two brothers-in-law.

"The Lord had me stay home alone and soon I would find out why. As I was packing, the Holy Spirit led me to Ken's suitcase and had me lift up the bottom of the inside of it to find an address book with over two pages of women's names and their descriptions. At first, I froze, as tears of unbelief welled up deep inside of me. *I wanted to run* (I felt like I had finally found my ticket out of a very unhappy marriage), but the still, small voice of the Spirit of God within constrained me. *"Remember, I'm in control,"* He said. *"How you handle this and the choices you make are critical. Choose to walk by faith, not your feelings, and your life will change."*

"I called a friend and placed myself under her accountability and received some wise counsel as to how to proceed. My husband arrived home shortly after that and with the book in hand, I asked him if this was happening now. He said, "yes." He just looked at me and said, "I am going to hell." "You know Jesus, will you please pray for me!"

"Those were perhaps the most honest words I have ever heard him say. So, I did pray and I asked God, "May *Your* will and not *mine* be done. I give this to You and it is now in Your hands." (My own feelings inside were screaming, "run, get out, this is your chance!" But I chose, by faith, to really mean what I had said in my prayer.)

"Immediately, Ken began to confess everything. He took the book from my hands, ran into the adjoining bathroom and lit it on fire. When he came back he said, "It is time to expose my sin."

"A dear pastor that we know came over that night and spent three hours with Ken out in the street. Later, the pastor asked me to come out and told me that, "Ken has just had a Damascus Road experience." I wouldn't have believed him, except that I had prayed those very same words for my husband many times. And in a prayer meeting just a month earlier, someone gave me a word for my husband, using "the Damascus Road" analogy. Then the pastor said to me, "God has heard your prayer. Ken was saved tonight and baptized out in that street." Well, you can imagine how I was feeling!

"The next few weeks involved a lot of pain, but an unfolding of the Glory of God like I have never seen before. Ken confessed to all the men that he is close to. He confessed to our four teenage children, my mom, sisters and two pastor friends that he was a false convert living a life headed for hell. He even named all his sins sparing the grossness of the details to protect their imaginations. Telling the children was the hardest of all. They each began to cry. They thought their dad *was* a Christian. But God's glory shined, even through this, and He began to heal all of our hearts.

"Eventually, Ken asked me to marry him again and our lives have never been the same. He now calls me from his car and holds the phone up to the marriage tapes he is listening to, so I can hear. For the first time in 19 years, we are experiencing the oneness in the Spirit that God so desires. We are continually in the Word and praying together. We have had more conversation in the past year than we've had in all our 19 years put together.  Our children are alive as never before.  I didn't realize till now that they, too, were dying.

"There is so much more to share, but God has given me a heart filled with the joy that is born out of pain, a great new love for my Savior and a hunger to know God's Love in an even deeper way.  Isn't He wonderful!"

(As an aside here:  Be careful not to put God in a "box."  Sometimes, in situations similar to Anna's, God might tell you to leave for your own safety, because He knows about dangerous extenuating factors towards you or your children.  The most important thing is to hear what God is telling you for *your* particular situation and then make the appropriate choices to follow Him.)

## Choices:  The Key to Our Christian Walk

What makes the above story so miraculous?  It's miraculous because, in spite of how Anna felt, in spite of what she thought and in spite of what she wanted, she chose to trust God and, by faith, do His will.  God then supernaturally changed her feelings to align with her choices and restored her marriage.  This story is miraculous because Anna made non-feeling choices that allowed God to intervene and thus, change the course of her life.

What would have happened had Anna chosen to follow her own justified feelings?  She would have immediately split with Ken and her story would have ended up like hundreds of others that we see and hear about today. Our choices are critical, because if we can learn to make choices by faith, they <u>can</u> *change the course of our lives*!

Naturally, even as Christians, we are still full of "self," our own natural thoughts, emotions and desires—especially in trials. Now, some of our hurts, unforgiveness, bitterness, and resentments *are* fully "justified" by the world's standards (i.e., the above example). But by God's standards, because we hold on to these things, mull them over in our minds and usually act upon them, these negative thoughts and emotions end up quenching God's Spirit in us. If we can learn to give our real feelings and thoughts over to God, like Anna did in the above example, and choose by faith alone to follow God's will, again like Anna, then He will align our feelings with the choices we have made and make us genuine, like with Anna.

Matthew 16:24 tells us that, "If any man will come after Me, *let him deny himself, take up his cross, and follow* Me."

To *deny* in the above Scripture does not mean to push down and bury our real feelings, nor does it mean to negate their existence. As Christians, many of us have been doing this, thinking we are not supposed to feel this way. But one of the beauties of the freedom that Christ has given us is that we can be honest with Him, acknowledge these things, confess and repent of them, give them over to Him and be free from them altogether. Thus, to deny simply means to *bar ourselves or to prevent ourselves from following what we naturally think and feel.* We're all human and we'll have these kinds of negative thoughts and feelings until we see Jesus.

Thus, it's important we look at these movers of our soul, call them for what they are so we will know exactly what we are dealing with and then, know how to give them over to the Lord. We must learn to "bar ourselves or prevent ourselves" from following what these negative elements of our lives are telling us, and instead, learn to give them to the Lord so we can be free to follow what He desires. (We will discuss each of these principles in more detail in future chapters.)

## Can We Make Choices We Don't Feel?

As humans, we are programmed from our birth to *feel* everything we choose. When we don't "feel" our choices, we don't think they're genuine. In God's kingdom, however, this is not the case. Born-again believers are the only ones who possess a supernatural authority (God's Word) within them to choose to go *against the tide* of "self"—what we think, feel and desire—because we're the only ones who possess a supernatural power (God's Spirit) within us to perform something different than what self wants, thinks and feels. Let me explain:

Certainly non-believers have a choice to do as they please. But none of them have the authority or the power to choose *to go against* how they feel or what they think because they don't possess another power source (another spirit) within them to perform anything different than what "self" tells them.

Therefore, even though they might desperately want to change and go a different direction, they don't possess an ability within them to do so. Thus, they really don't have any other choice but to follow what their own thoughts, emotions and desires are telling them. (Ephesians 4:17-18) Christians, on the other hand, do! We don't have to be carried on by the tide of emotion, since we have God's Spirit within us; this Spirit not only gives us the authority to choose God's will, but also His power to perform that will in our lives.

In other words, believers and nonbelievers alike can choose whatever they wish. We all can make non-feeling choices. *But only Christians have the supernatural power and ability of God within them to be able to implement those faith choices in their lives.*

## A Classic Example: Did You Tell Him Off?

Here's a perfect example:

One Christmas, years ago, we rented a house at Lake Tahoe for two weeks. Our intention was to be totally alone—just our family. What a dream. We would be together for two whole weeks, playing games and reading. I could even work on my upcoming speech for a new class I was teaching. I couldn't wait! My own mom and dad were visiting my brother in San Francisco, and we could have easily invited them down to Tahoe for a few days. But Chuck had said no, this was to be our own special vacation—just our family—with no intrusions.

One fabulous week went by. Our family never seemed closer. There was no T.V. and no outside influences to disturb our unity. We all read, talked, lied around and did our own thing. It was absolutely wonderful!

Then one morning, out of the blue, Chuck announces to all of us, "I hope you don't mind, but I have invited a business associate and his wife up here to join us for a few days." Well, you could have knocked me over dead. Chuck is the one who had made such a big deal about having no outside interferences! If I had known he would allow company, I would have much rather had my own folks!

"How long are these business people going to stay?" I asked. "Well, as long as they want, I guess," he responded. He had actually left the invitation open ended! At that moment, in the flesh I could have killed him! I was so upset and so angry!

Here we weren't supposed to have anything or anyone disturb our family or our privacy, and now we're not only having an outsider over (someone I had never even met before), but they were staying for who knows how long! I just couldn't believe Chuck would do something like that. I needn't tell you how I wrestled with anger and bitterness towards him. How would you have responded?

Later, when I was sharing this story in one of my seminars, someone stood up right in the middle of the story and asked, "Well, Nancy, did you tell Chuck off right then and there?"

I laughed and responded to this precious sister, "Man, I wanted to. It's our natural human tendency to immediately tell the other person how we feel, but that's not always what God would have us do. So, no, I didn't tell Chuck off right then, and there were two good reasons why I didn't: 1) Chuck had already extended an invitation to this couple, so it was already a fact that they were coming, and I couldn't do anything about it by throwing a tantrum; and 2) I wasn't clean. I was full of my own wild emotions and uncontrolled thoughts. Therefore, I had to first deal with my own anger and resentment before I could take a stand in God's Love with Chuck."

Later, when I was clean (after I had confessed and given God all my feelings) and my emotions were back in place, I did tell Chuck in Love how disappointed I was that he had gone against what he had promised. I know he heard because all the kids had already gone to him and shared the very same thing.

So, there's definitely a time when we can share how we really feel, but we must make sure it's done in God's Love and in His Character and not our own. Otherwise, we'll end up deeper in the pits than when we started.

The day after Christmas, we heard from the couple that they were on their way. In order to prepare for their arrival we had to: rearrange the children's rooms so the guests could have a room of their own; make a special trip to the grocery store to buy extra food; and, clean the house as you would for company. So much energy and fuss goes into having guests, especially when they are business acquaintances and you have never met them before. These were all things that I shouldn't have had to do on *my* vacation.

I will never forget the day they arrived! Our girls were watching for them out the window and all of a sudden they yelled, "Mom, here they are! And Mom, they have brought all of their kids!" At that moment, if Chuck had been close enough, I think I would have strangled him! This now made 12 people to feed three times a day, clean up after, and entertain for who knows how long! And all this on *my* vacation!

I can't tell you the number of times I went to the Lord, frustrated and crying, saying, "You know I came up here to work on my speech for the next *Way of Agape* seminar, and now, Lord, I can't!" But you know what He would always answer? "I want you to work on the material for your next seminar, but I want you to "live" it first! I am giving you a perfect opportunity to glorify Me and be full of My Life to these people." I replied in all honesty, I'd much rather "write" about it than "live" it!

Constantly, I had to make a choice as to which way I would go. I could make an emotional choice to follow what my anger, resentment, and bitterness were telling me (to tell Chuck off, put on a smiling "face" for the guests, and get rid of them as soon as possible). Or I could make a faith choice and follow what God was telling me to do, which was to give Him my hurts and anger, and know that He somehow would give me the Love, grace and strength I needed to genuinely put Chuck and these new people first.

Don't let me kid you—it wasn't easy!  Making choices you don't feel, and especially ones you don't want to make, is extremely difficult.  But as I kept choosing over and over again to follow God and go His Way, He was faithful to take away my anger and resentment, and fill me with His Love— not only for Chuck, but also for these people.

The business associate and his wife turned out to be a delightful Jewish couple.  They even taught us some Hebrew and answered many of our questions about the Old Testament.  We ended up having a marvelous four days with them.  It was during this time that God sparked the idea for the *Be Ye Transformed* study.

Can you imagine what kind of an impression I would have made on these people if I had chosen <u>not</u> to surrender myself and follow God?  I would have been full of my own hurts and bitterness with a plastic smile over my face, pretending to be happy and glad, but showing forth "self life" and not God's Life at all.  One of those "phony-baloney Christians."  You know they would have sensed it.

"...ye are like unto whited sepulchres, which indeed appear beautiful outward, but are within full of dead men's bones, and of all uncleanness." (Matthew 23:27)

Faith choices or "contrary choices" (I like this latter term because these kinds of choices are definitely *contrary to what I feel, think and desire*), are the only ones that can free us from ourselves and unleash all of God's Power to come to our aid.

As Christians, we can be totally honest with God and admit, "I don't love this person anymore. In fact, I really can't stand him right now. But, by faith, I give these negative thoughts and feelings to You, for I know I have Your authority to claim, like Jesus did in Matthew 26:39, "...*not my will* [not my natural feelings and desires], *but Thine.*" Then I can be assured that (since I am a cleansed vessel) God will align my feelings with that choice, make me genuine and perform His will in and through me.

To me, this is one of the most incredible gifts God has given us. We don't have to "feel" our choices, we simply have to be willing to make them. God, then, in His perfect timing and way, does the rest.

## Our Goal and Purpose as Christians

The basic goal and purpose for all of our lives as Christians is to be conformed into the image of Christ so that *His Life* and *His Love* from our hearts can flow freely out into our lives. (Romans 8:29) God wants us to love with His Love; He wants us to think with His Wisdom and to function on His power and ability. He wants us to be *at one* with Him, so all that is seen through us is Him. Then others will want what we have and the Gospel will have a chance to be truly passed on.

Most Christians would agree that we've not been called simply to gain knowledge *about* Christ, but to gain more of His Life to give to others.  Most understand that true Christianity is not about "head knowledge," but about Christ's Life being personally experienced and then, passed on. *The problem is, most Christians don't know how to make that happen!*

We don't know how to make choices to yield ourselves to the Lord, so that His Life <u>can</u> come forth. What happens instead, is that when we get hurt or offended, we end up consumed with our own negative thoughts and feelings, which in turn, quenches God's Spirit in our hearts and blocks His Life from coming forth.  Then, the life that shows forth in our souls is not God's, as it should be, but our own *self-life*. Consequently, rather than bring people closer to the Lord, our fleshly behavior pushes them away and the Gospel is unable to be passed on.

## An Example:  Searching For A Reason To Live

Many years ago, a woman called our office who was searching for a reason to go on living.  She had been a Christian for about 11 years, but didn't have the slightest idea as to how to experience Christ's Love, either for herself or for others.  She had read Romans 8:29, but didn't know how to apply it personally to her life. Thus, she never saw God's Wisdom at work in her relationships, nor experienced walking in the Power of His Spirit.  Without personally experiencing these things—His Life at work in her and through her—she had no basis to understand what true Christianity was all about.  Up until then, it had all been "rules and regulations."

When I questioned her about laying her life down to God and committing everything to Him, she said, "Of course, I've done that!"  However, when I asked her about making faith choices or non-feeling choices in order to do this, she had no idea what I was talking about.  *There was the problem!*  Knowing how to make faith choices to yield ourselves to God, regardless of how we feel, is absolutely imperative to experiencing the abundant Life.  Without this step of saying, "Not my will, but Thine," it's impossible to genuinely yield our lives to God, unless, of course, we bury our real feelings, only prolonging the emotional explosion. (Again, we will cover this principle in more detail in future chapters.)  Doing God's will goes hand in hand with making choices we don't feel.  We can't do one without the other.

For example:  How many of us "feel like" surrendering ourselves to God when our flesh is screaming just the opposite?  None of us do, especially when it means dying to our own desires! We're still human and we still naturally value our "selves."  That's why Jesus tells us we must learn to *deny self, pick up our cross and follow Him.* (Matthew 16:24)   In other words, we must learn to *get beyond ourselves*!  This only occurs by making choices by faith, not feelings.

The above lady has now rejected Christianity and is out in the world, seeing an analyst and searching for happiness elsewhere.  I asked her if she had found what she was looking for and she yelled back at me, "Are you kidding?  I am more angry, hopeless and empty now than I ever was before!"  She went on to admit that she hates herself and cannot accept the fact that God still loves her.

I believe there are thousands of Christians out there, just like this precious woman, who have tried to live the Christian life by their own natural love, wisdom and abilities, and just like this woman, have failed miserably.  They have never heard of faith choices or contrary choices or non-feeling choices, and thus they have simply gotten tired of the hypocrisy and quit trying.  Many of these wonderful people have strived for so long to be "model" Christians—doing, doing, doing—and yet, like the above woman, never really experiencing Christ's real Life at work in or through them.  Thus, they have finally just given up.  *The tragic part is that they have never really experienced true Christianity at all!*

Therefore, it's essential not only to know what God's goal and purpose is for our lives as Christians— that Christ may be formed *in* us and lived out *through us*—but also to know how to make faith choices so that goal may be reached!

## God Wants Us to Exchange Lives

Consequently, being a Christian doesn't mean simply "copying" or "imitating" Jesus' Life, but *exchanging lives* with Him!  We give Him ours; He then gives us His.  In other words, He wants to replace us with Himself.  He wants to exchange our image for the image we were created to bear from the very beginning, which is His image.

The dictionary tells us that an image is an exact likeness of something. (Hebrews 1:3) It's a visible representation or reproduction of the form of a person. As we allow God to conform us more and more into His Image and His Likeness, it will be His Image and His Life that we'll portray to the world and not our own.

Galatians 2:20 validates this, "I am crucified with Christ: nevertheless I live; yet not I, but *Christ liveth in me*: and the life which I now live in the flesh I live by the faith of the Son of God, Who loved me, and gave Himself for me."

Thus, as Christians, it's not our job to fix up, repair or mend our "self life." That's what psychology teaches! *God wants us to learn how to make choices to set that "self" aside so that Jesus can live His Life out through us.* Again, He wants us to "deny ourselves, pick up our crosses and follow Him." Again, "deny" does not mean hide or bury our real feelings. It's imperative that we allow God to expose and bring up our real thoughts so that He can then replace them with His own. In Chapter Seven, we'll learn exactly how we are to do this.

People often ask me, "What is the best thing I can do for my unbelieving spouse and my wayward kids," or "my wayward spouse and my unbelieving kids?" "What book should I get?" "What tapes should I listen to?" "What class would you recommend?" My answer is always simple: *Live Christ's Life! Live His Love!* Show that it works for you in the bad times, as well as the good times.

The first Commandment tells us we are to love the Lord our God with all our heart, mind and soul. Loving God—totally giving ourselves over to Him—simply means exchanging ourselves (our own thoughts, emotions and desires) for His Self (His Love, His Thoughts, and His Power).

## "It Doesn't Matter What We Look Like"

Here's a perfect example of how this exchange of life occurs:

A few years ago, Dutch, a Viet Nam veteran, came into our ministry offices looking for Chuck and me. This dear man had lost an arm, a hand, an ear and an eye in the war, and had many other physical disabilities besides. When he saw us, he burst into tears, grabbed the two of us and began to tell us his incredible story.

He had been a Christian for over 18 years, but had struggled for most of those years trying to find meaning and purpose for his life as a Christian. Understandably, he had suffered severe marital and relationship problems, financial problems, as well as many other serious physical problems. He told us how he had become a part of several church outreaches, trying to find personal fulfillment. But, he said, "*something was always missing.*"

Then someone handed him *The Way of Agape*
book on loving the way God designed; he said his
life changed forever.  Through that little book Dutch
learned that God's purpose in choosing him was to
conform him into His image—to exchange lives with
Him—so that His (God's) Life could flow *through
him* to others.  Dutch told us how the Lord began to
work this message of the exchanged life into his heart
and how he was seeing himself genuinely change
from the inside out.  He said he had finally found
what his real meaning and purpose was as a Christian:
*to be a cleansed vessel so that God can live His Life
out through him.*  Dutch then went on to say, *"The
neat part is, that it doesn't matter what that vessel
looks like.  The important thing is that God's Life is
reflected through it."*

## Exchanging Lives Doesn't Happen Naturally

Unfortunately, this exchange of life doesn't happen
automatically.  How I wish it did!  Wouldn't it just be
great if we could push a button and automatically
Christ's Life would be out there.  I wouldn't even
mind if I had to choose only once in the morning (like
getting dressed) and then stay filled with Him all day
long.  But, this isn't the case.  We must choose every
moment of every day, to deny ourselves, pick up our
cross and follow Him.

Just because we are Christians does not mean that
God's Life will *automatically* flow from our hearts
out into our lives.  It won't!  *It all depends upon
our moment-by-moment choices!*  As we said, even
as Christians we are still full of self, especially in

trials. And the fears, hurts and justified feelings that we choose to hang on to (just to make us feel better), will end up quenching God's Life in our hearts and preventing us from reflecting His real Life.

Now, some of these feelings that we experience are fully justified by the world's standards as in Anna's story at the beginning of this chapter, but if we mull them over in our minds or bury them, these negative emotions will quench God's Spirit in our hearts and separate us from His Life.

Lest I confuse you, let me explain exactly what I mean when I say *"separate us from God's Life."* If we are believers, then we always have God's Life in our hearts. Romans 8:38-39 states that "nothing separates us from His Love (and His Life)," and 1 Corinthians 13:8 tells us, "His Love never stops coming." However, if God's Spirit is quenched because of something we have chosen to hold on to that is not of faith, then that Life of God (in our hearts) will not be able to flow out into our lives (or our souls). Technically, yes, we still have God's Life in our hearts, but practically, until we deal with that sin and self (confess it, repent of it and give it over to Him), we will *not* experience His Life in our souls. Thus, Isaiah 59:2 is also true for a Christian: "Your iniquities have separated between you and your God, and your sins have hid His face from you, that he will not hear."

(Note: The original negative thought is not what separates us from the Lord. It's what we choose to do with that ungodly thought that makes it sin or not. In other words, when we choose to nurture, entertain

and continually mull over ungodly thoughts or ones
that are not of faith—rather than give them to God—
then they <u>will</u> become sin and they <u>will</u> separate us
from His life.  We will discuss this principle further
in Chapter Six.)

If, however, we choose to surrender our negative
thinking to the Lord and become a cleansed channel
for His use, He then will be able to pour His Life out
through us.

Can you imagine what our marriages, our families
and our churches would be like if more of us did this
on a regular basis?  Scripture tells us that the world will
know we are Christians not by our words, our signs,
our doctrines, or even our knowledge of Scripture,
but simply "*by being open vessels genuinely showing
forth Christ's Life.*" (John 13:35)

## Reflecting God's Life Involves a Choice

But, again, in order to genuinely reflect His Life,
we must constantly make a choice—the choice to
allow God to use us.  Again, just because we are
Christians does <u>not</u> mean that Christ's Life will
automatically flow through us.  It won't!  It's only
as we make choices to deny ourselves (set ourselves
aside) and be open, that His Life can manifest itself.

When we do this, we're not saying: "I will love
this person if it kills me."  We're saying, "I choose
to set my self aside (all my thoughts, emotions and
desires that are contrary to God's) so that <u>God</u> can
love this person *through* me."    It's God's Love;

it's His wisdom; and it's His ability to perform these things in our lives. A whole different way of thinking...

Thus, only *our willpower* is involved (not our emotions, our thoughts or our desires), which, of course, is completely opposite from our natural, emotional way of loving. Thus, much of the time we won't "feel" like making these kinds of choices. However, as we will see throughout this book, it's absolutely essential that we know how to make faith choices, *because they determine whose life will be lived in our souls—God's or our own.* Choices we make to follow God's will, regardless of how we feel or what we think, allow God's Life from our hearts to flow out into our lives. Choices we make to follow what we feel and what we want, quench God's Life in our hearts and force us to show forth our self-life.

## Are You Willing To "Go Against The Tide?"

The question the Lord continually asks us is: "Are you willing?" Are you willing to go *against the tide* and choose, by faith, to follow Him?

Are you willing to tear up that long list of justified hurts that that other person has done to you and choose, instead, to do God's will? Can you unconditionally forgive that family member, that Christian friend or that business associate who has humiliated and betrayed you over and over again, and for the hundredth time, choose to give yourself totally over to God?

If you are a believer, then you have the authority and the supernatural power to do so. The question is, will you?

Please understand that it's totally impossible to do the above things in our own strength. Unconditionally loving and forgiving those who have hurt, rejected or betrayed us is completely opposite to our own emotional way of thinking and acting. Remember Anna. Only God can do these things *through* us. And it's only when we make faith choices to yield ourselves to Him that He can manifest Himself through us.

The secret, the key, the truth that has changed my life, and that can radically change yours, is learning *how* to make choices that literally take away your negative thoughts and emotions, and in their place, be filled up with His. Again, we don't have to feel these choices. We must only be willing to make them. God, then, will align the "movers of soul" to match the choices we have made, make us genuine and restore our joy.

John 12:24 validates that, "Except a grain of wheat fall into the ground and die, it abideth alone; but if it die, it bringeth forth much fruit."

# Chapter Two
## *Our Free Will*

God has given man a free will, much like His own. Our free will is the most important element of our make-up, because within that will lies the *power to choose*: to choose to follow what God desires or follow what our own emotions and desires are telling us. Our will is the master of all of our faculties and upon it everything else depends. Our will controls our reason, our intelligence, our emotions and all our abilities. In other words, *our will is the "gate" through which all things must pass and the bridge over which our faith must travel.*

Now, the reason our will is so very important to God, is that unless we choose by an act of our will to allow Him to accomplish His will through us, He is unable to do so. Now, of course, God can do as He pleases, however, in order for Him to use us as He desires, *we must cooperate with Him.* God has not set Himself up as our Divine Dictator, but rather as our loving Discipler, and thus, He has given us the free choice to either follow Him or deny Him. This is a choice we not only make once, but constantly. In other words, the Lord desires that we render back to Him that which we have so long claimed as our own—namely, our own will.

Life, therefore, is really just a series of ongoing choices. For the non-believer, it's a daily choice between good and evil; for the believer, it's a moment-by-moment choice to either follow our own will and desires, or to say, like Jesus, "Not my will, but Thine." (Matthew 26:39)

## An Example: It's Worth a Million Dollars

We all have many examples in our own lives of the consequences of these two kinds of choices. Here's a classic situation I was faced with many years ago:

I had been praying that God would make me a more supportive wife for Chuck in his business. Now, that's an easy commitment to make in the prayer closet. It's quite another thing, however, to trust God to do it in my actions. God was going to give me a perfect opportunity to see what I would choose.

At this particular time, I was teaching *The Way of Agape*. Tammy, a friend of mine, volunteered to watch 10-year old Michelle for me on my teaching days. One time Tammy decided to take all the kids to the beach. My Michelle is very fair, and on that particular day Tammy forgot to bring sun screen. When I picked Michelle up that night, she was "burnt to a crisp."

The following afternoon she seemed better, so I decided to take a chance and go grocery shopping. Michelle acted fine until my cart was completely filled, and then she began to lean over the front of the grocery cart, moaning and groaning about her sunburn. I needed the groceries desperately, so I decided to gamble and see if I could check out quickly! Well, as you know, whenever you're in a hurry, it always ends up taking forever.

We got up to the check-out stands and there were at least five people in every line. Michelle, by this time, was leaning over the front of the cart, crying softly. People began to stare at us. I'm sure some of them thought I must be beating her because they couldn't see her sunburn. Terribly flustered and embarrassed, I felt like leaving the groceries and running out of the store, but I really needed the milk and butter that were at the bottom of the cart.

Finally getting through the line and out of the store, we flew home. As I was driving, I was thinking to myself, "I can't wait to get home, put Michelle to bed, wash my filthy hair, get comfortable, put my feet up, and read all evening." I was totally bushed!

When we pulled up to our street, a detour sign had been posted because it had been dug up for repairs. Now, that detour was two miles out of my way and poor Michelle was still whining in the back seat. By the time I finally got home, I was absolutely frazzled.

As I was carrying the first grocery bags down the steps with Michelle on my arm, I could hear the phone shrilly ringing. I dropped the bags, fumbled for my keys, and finally reached the phone on the ninth ring. It was Chuck's secretary, and she seemed frantic. "Nancy, where have you been? We almost sent the police after you!"

With that, Chuck got on the phone and said, "Honey, don't say a word, just quickly get dressed in your fanciest outfit. We are being driven by a chauffeur up to Scandia, a fancy restaurant in Los Angeles tonight, and it could be worth a million dollars to the company. But you need to be here by 5 pm sharp!" With that, he hung up! I looked at the clock. It was now twenty minutes to five!

CHOICE POINT: Emotional choice or a faith choice? Which way am I going to choose? Emotional choice would have me scream, stamp my feet, call him back and declare, "I'm sorry, but there's just no way I can do it. I'm a mess; Michelle's a mess; groceries are still in the car; dinner's not made, etc.!" Or, am I going to make a faith choice and choose what I know to be God's Will by simply trusting Him to get me ready and there on time?

Lisa had come home by that time and had heard all the commotion. I took Michelle and Lisa by the hands and said, "We really need to pray for Mommy." In that prayer, I told God it was impossible to do what Chuck had just asked. It was now a quarter to five. His office was at least 10 minutes away, even without the rush hour traffic. Nevertheless, I told God I was willing to do whatever He wanted me to.

With that, little Michelle said, "Mommy, don't worry about me, I'll just go lie down and rest." Michelle had never before lain down of her own free will! Lisa then chimed in, "Mom, don't worry about the food. I'll bring in the groceries and fix dinner for the two of us." Lisa had never, up until that time, offered to bring in groceries or to make dinner. This was a first! It was a miracle!

That left me free to concentrate on me. I flew upstairs, called Grandma to babysit, took a one-minute shower, did what I could with my wild hair, got dressed, and would you believe I made it to Chuck's office by five past five, rush-hour traffic and all.

We didn't get the contract, but I'll tell you, Chuck sure noticed and appreciated my supportiveness. And I experienced God's faithfulness to perform His Life through me, regardless of my emotions.

## Our Free Choice

Our Christian life is <u>not</u> determined by our circumstances, our church attendance, our social standing, our finances or even our belief systems, but *the character of our Christian life is determined by the daily choices we make.*

Sin isn't birthed in our mind or in our body; it's begun within our will! God has given us a fearful and awesome responsibility with our "free will," because what we choose determines the degree of our sanctification. *Faith choices* allow God's Life from our hearts to flow out into our lives; whereas, *emotional choices* quench God's Life and block it from coming forth.

Scripture tells us that when we are "born again" we not only receive a new spirit and a new heart, but we also receive a new supernatural willpower. This new willpower is not only God's *authority* enabling us to choose His will over our own, but also His *power* to carry out and perform that will in our lives. As Philippians 2:13 says, "For it is God Which worketh in you both *to will* and *to do,* of His good pleasure."

In other words, our new willpower gives us the authority and power of God to *"go against the tide"*— to set ourselves aside and follow Him, regardless of how we feel, what we want or what we think. *Our free choice is the critical crossroads of our lives.*

## Exousia

The Greek word for this "free choice" decision is *exousia* which means "it is permitted." *Exousia* means we are permitted to choose something we don't feel. It means we have the authority and the word of the person in charge to do this (which is God), and we also have His power and ability to make it happen in our lives. What this is saying is: as Christians, we have the delegated authority and power of God to choose to "relinquish ourselves" and do what He wants, or, to "hold on to ourselves" and do what we please.

Jesus states in John 10:17-18, "Therefore doth My Father love Me, because I lay down My life, that I might take it again. No man taketh it from Me, but I lay it down of Myself. I have power [*exousia*] to lay it down, and I have power [*exousia*] to take it again."

God is the one who gives us the supernatural power to override our own negative thoughts, feelings and desires [i.e., to "forbid self"], and to say, like Jesus did, "Not my will [my own emotional desires], but Thine." (Matthew 26:39) In other words, choose to *go against the tide*.

In Matthew 16:19, Jesus promises, "I will give unto thee the keys of the kingdom of heaven: and whatsoever thou shalt bind on earth shall be bound in heaven: and whatsoever thou shalt loose on earth shall be loosed in heaven."

Now, we always associate this Scripture with the enemy (binding and loosing him by the Holy Spirit). But in a personal sense, to bind literally means to "prohibit or forbid self" and to loose means to "permit or to allow self." This Scripture is saying that we possess the authority and the power of God (within our willpower as Christians), to choose to either "forbid self" (relinquish, surrender, and set self aside) and walk after the Spirit, or the power to "allow self" (let self reign) and walk after the flesh.

(For further study and more Scriptural references of this material, please see the book *Way of Agape* Chapter 12.)

## Contrary Choices

I call the former kind of choice *a faith choice, a non-feeling choice* or *a contrary choice*. They are contrary choices because, as we said before, they are contrary to how we naturally feel, what we think and what we want, but nevertheless, they are valid because God has given us the authority to make them.  1 Corinthians 7:37 validates that in Christ we have "...power [authority] over [our] own will..." (John 10:18)

Thus, we can be honest with the Lord and say: "I really don't like this person.  I don't want to forgive him.  I don't want to love him.  He's not my friend!" But, then we can make a *contrary choice* and say, "Nevertheless, not my will, but Thine."  In other words, "I'll do what You want me to, regardless of how I feel," because I know You will change my feelings in Your timing and You will perform Your will in my life.

What's so incredible about making these kinds of *contrary choices* is that God does, in His timing and in His Way, not only change our negative thoughts and emotions to align with what we have chosen, but also He restores our joy.  In other words, if we are just willing to make the right choices, He will give us the Love, wisdom and power we need to go on as if nothing has happened.

## An Example:  Mother-in-law Troubles

A perfect example:   Many years ago, I received a letter from a dear friend of mine, explaining a very difficult situation she'd had with her mother-in-law.  Carol explained that if she hadn't known how to make "contrary choices," she could have easily "ended up devastated."

This is what she wrote:

"My mother-in-law had come for a two-and-a-half week visit at Christmas time. During this time, the Lord had allowed a number of pressure points to surface in our relationship, pressures that can so easily occur, especially during the busy holiday season. The enemy continually sought to divide us.

"I had been planning to give my husband a special surprise gift for his 50th birthday coming up shortly after the holidays. In order to give him this gift, I needed to trust the Lord for two things: child care for one week for my 7-year old daughter; and $700, which I did not have. Within one day, the Lord provided the child care.

"The day before Christmas, my mother-in-law asked what I was going to do for my husband's birthday. When I told her about the surprise, she volunteered to pay for half of it. My first response was to decline her generous offer, knowing that she was on a limited income, but since she was insistent, I believed it was the Lord's way of answering my prayer. I was still a bit uneasy about it, however.

"Later that same day, my mother-in-law came to me and said, "Well, when are you going to tell him about his birthday gift?" Now, I had it all planned in my mind how I was going to surprise my husband on his actual birthday. When I told her this, she became very hurt, letting me know that since she was the one who was going to pay for half of it, she should be able to tell her son now, since she would not be here on his birthday.

"Self" screamed inside, "It's not fair! I planned this surprise! I didn't want her money anyway!" But, I knew deep within my spirit, however, that I was to do as she wished.

"I relinquished my desires to God and asked Him to give me the grace I needed. It was so exciting—God not only gave me His Words to tell her, but He also changed my feelings, softened my voice, and filled me with His Love for her.

"I knew God was in this because it was no longer important to me to have "my way." What became preeminent was, "Will I choose to be and do what God wants?"

"Well, she <u>did</u> tell my husband, and she <u>did</u> spoil my surprise, but God <u>did</u> deliver me. He took away my hurt and disappointment, and replaced them with His Love in my heart. We ended up having a great birthday week."

---------------------

Therefore, the *choice to relinquish the negative feelings to God is ours;* but the responsibility to change those feelings is God's. The fact is, there's no way we can ever change our feelings by ourselves. God is the One who will be faithful to make us genuine by the time we need to do whatever it is He has asked. In other words, God promises to produce His Love and all the fruit of the Spirit needed in our lives, if we simply make the right choice.

(One important thing to keep in mind: the deeper the wound (i.e., the longer that arrow has been *in us*), the longer it seems to take for our feelings to align with our choices.)

## Our Choice Is Where Sin Begins

Therefore, the battle between the flesh and Spirit is either won or lost in the area of our willpower. In other words, *our choice is where sin begins*. Our choice to follow our own thoughts and emotions over what God has prompted is where the Spirit gets quenched and sin results. (1 Thessalonians 5:19; Ephesians 4:30)

Romans 14:23 expresses it perfectly: "Whatsoever [choice] is not of faith is sin." Also, James 4:17: "To him that knoweth to do good, and doeth it not [chooses not to do it], to him it is sin."

Consequently, any choice or any unwillingness to obey God, causes the door of our hearts to slam on Him—and that's sin. Now, having the original, ungodly or negative thought is not sin. We're all human, and we're all going to have bad thoughts until we see Jesus. The sin enters when we choose *to follow* what those negative thoughts are prompting us to do <u>over</u> what God is telling us to do! The Spirit gets quenched even when we simply entertain, mull over or bury those thoughts rather than giving them to Him. This is where sin enters and self life takes over.

## An Example: "I Thought He Was Divorced!"

Here's a perfect example.    Debbie    began a relationship with Richard thinking that he was divorced.  After all, that's what he had told her and she had no reason to doubt him.  She fell hard for Richard and when he told her that he "loved her" and "wanted to marry her," she was absolutely thrilled.

The truth, however, was that Richard's divorce was <u>not</u> yet complete.  He still needed a final decree from his church to make it legal.  When Richard's wife found out about Debbie, she backed off of the divorce and began to take actions towards reconciliation.  Richard, by this time, had lost all feelings for his wife, so he was a bit taken back when all this transpired.  He felt it was too late for them to work things out and besides, he had fallen in love with Debbie and wanted to marry her.

In spite of his wife's advances, Richard continued to pursue Debbie saying, "my feelings for you have not changed. I think about you every day. You make me feel valued and appreciated and I feel my life, at last, has some direction.  I want to marry you."

Debbie was devastated when she found out that Richard had been lying to her—that he wasn't really divorced yet. Her decision became clear, even though it was the hardest one she'd ever had to make. She loved Richard passionately and truly wanted to become his wife, but after praying extensively about it, she knew exactly what she had to do. Here's her letter to Richard:

"Dearest Richard, the content of this letter is not the response that you are hoping for, but I pray that you will understand why my decision is what it is... While I sympathize with you in a worldly way, I must stress that to be born again Christians, we live *in* the world, but we should not be *of* the world. Decisions we feel and often make as Christians are *not* always in the direction that the Lord wants us to go. We have a free will. We constantly come across situations that cause us to make choices. We can choose the easy, emotional and worldly way, or we can choose the sometimes harder way: to follow God.

*"I have learned that when I make a faith choice (a non-feeling choice) based on Scriptural references, and not on my emotional and heart's desires, it brings about a much closer relationship with the Lord.*

"We should look at each situation we encounter as a chance to strengthen our faith. For example, how much time did you spend in prayer requesting your wife's change of heart? A lot, I assume. Yet, when she *did* change her mind, you did not believe for one minute that it could be of God... She wanted you back and you flatly refused without giving her—the wife you once chose—a second chance. No one would have expected you to jump right back in full on, but given time and prayer, you might, at least, have had the chance to show God that you were willing to put Him before your *own* wants and desires. Then, He would have given you the Love you needed and once had. *Unfortunately, the bitterness, the anger and the hurt you feel towards your wife and the* *self-pity you express, seem to have hardened your heart against everything that is <u>not</u> your own will!*

"My feelings for you are very deep and I was so looking forward to becoming your wife, but I had to make a choice between you and God (between my feelings and doing the right thing). The only choice I can make is to follow the Lord.

"My prayer is that you will bury the feelings you still have for me and turn to the Lord with an open heart, confess and repent of the sin we both have committed and then, perhaps, you can think about rebuilding your family. May the Lord lead and guide you..."

What an incredibly hard choice Debbie had to make, the ultimate choice—between what she yearned for more than anything else in the world and what she knew was God's will. But she made the right choice—she chose to follow God over and above her own feelings, and I know that the Lord will restore to her a hundred-fold all that she chose to give up.

## God's Will or Self Will: That's the Question

Thus, we are constantly faced with two choices. We can make a *"faith choice,"* regardless of how we feel and follow what God desires by saying, "Not my will, but Thine." (Matthew 26:39) Or we can make an *"emotional choice,"* to follow our own thoughts and emotions over what God has asked and trust in our own ability to perform it in our lives.

God's will or self will, that's the question. Either we allow God to will His will through us—that which is pleasing to Him, or we will our own will—that which is pleasing to us. Are you willing to lay down all you want, think, and feel (like Debbie did), so that God's will can be performed through you? Or are you like Richard, unable to go against the tide and hardened against everything that is <u>not</u> your own will?

Loving God with all our willpower is the *key* to walking by the Spirit. It's binding our wills with His and becoming one will, regardless of what is going on in our lives. It's saying, "I don't feel like it, I don't understand it, and I don't want to do it, but nevertheless, not my will, but Thine. I know I have Your authority to make this kind of contrary choice and I know You will give me the power to perform it in my life."

It's interesting because the word *humility* actually means putting God and what He wants above our own needs. In other words, humility says, "not my will, but Thine." Whereas, the essence of pride is "I will." "I want my will, not Yours!" The Greek word for humility comes from the root *phren* which means "to rein in or to overcome." Overcoming simply means making faith choices or non-feeling choices that prevail over what our own thoughts, emotions and desires are urging us to do. It's allowing God's Spirit to control us instead. It's noteworthy that 1 John 5:4 tells us that faith (which is simply a series of choices) is the "victory that overcomes the world."

May God give us the humility to bring into captivity our own sin and self, so that Christ can be formed in us and passed on through us.

## The War

Romans 6:12-13 instructs, "Let not sin therefore reign in your mortal body, that ye should obey it in the lusts thereof. Neither yield ye your members as instruments of unrighteousness unto sin: but yield yourselves unto God, as those that are alive from the dead, and your members as instruments of righteousness unto God."

And verse 16 tells us, "Know ye not, that to whom ye yield yourselves servants to obey, his servants ye are to whom ye obey; whether of sin unto death, or of obedience unto righteousness?" And finally, verse 19, "...for as ye have [in the past] yielded your members servants to uncleanness and to iniquity unto iniquity; even so now yield your members servants to righteousness unto holiness."

This Scripture confirms that we do have a constant choice as to whom we will yield our members. Will we yield them to God to do His will, or will we yield them to "self" (our own emotions) to do our own will?

This is the constant choice we will face a hundred times a day, every day, for the rest of our Christian life. And, these choices are what determine whose life will be lived in our soul: God's or our own. God has all the Love, all the Wisdom and all the Power we need. The choice, however, to be a cleansed vessel through which He can pour these things, is always ours.

Therefore, the war that goes on within us between the *Power of God* and the *power of sin* is <u>not</u> in our hearts, as I used to believe and teach, but in our souls and bodies, i.e., the flesh. Romans 7:23 validates this, "But I see another law in my members [body], warring against the law of my mind [Law of the Spirit] and bringing me into captivity to the law of sin [power of sin] in my members." Recognizing this and bringing the flesh into captivity by choosing to put off the "old man" so that God's Life can come forth, is what the sanctification process is all about.

Paul tells us early in Romans 6:6-7 that since our old, evil heart life (our old man) has been done away with at our new birth, the power of sin's hold on the flesh has *already* been destroyed and we have already been freed from sin. In other words, Christ in our heart is now the overcoming power to free us from this struggle. And if we choose to surrender ourselves to Him, then we can, in His Strength, overcome whatever the "flesh" is urging us to do, and choose instead, by faith, to be filled with His Spirit.

Are you willing to set aside what you think, what you want, and what you feel to do what God wants? Or will you yield to your own hurts, emotions and desires?

Jeremiah 21:8 explains our constant choice, "Behold, I set before you the way of life [by making faith choices], and the way of death [by making emotional choices]." Which way will you choose, power of life or death?

# Chapter Three
## *Our New Supernatural Willpower*

Naomi was a victim of sexual abuse as a child. Throughout her life, even as a Christian, a wife and mom, the pain and desperation from that experience has been overwhelming, and she has continually battled despair and depression. Along the way, Naomi tried numerous Christian therapists, Alanon, Adult Children of Alcoholics, etc., but because she couldn't see God's hand in any of them, she stopped. She always knew *something* was missing! Sooner or later her symptoms of anxiety and depression would again resume. Her family doctor just thought it was stress, but she and her husband, Phil, knew better.

In February of last year, Naomi had a complete mental breakdown. God kept her safe, even though she tried to end her life. Phil, who works at the sheriff's department, was across town when he heard about his wife's collapse. He rushed home to be at her side, to love her, to care for her and to keep her from trying the same thing again. God finally rescued her from the valley of death. Confusion had permeated her mind, but through the loving arms of her husband and friends, God showed her that she could, if she really wanted to, be healed completely and never have to fear losing her sanity again.

*The key, however, was that she would have to "choose" every single day, and occasionally many times a day, to go God's way.* That was the missing link in all those other therapies: choosing to acknowledge her depressed thoughts, and then giving them over to God. She found when she made those faith choices, with God's help, she could go on with her life, be an instrument for *His* use and *He* was faithful to align her feelings with her choices.

"There will always be a battle for my mind," Naomi says, "but I don't have to fear the enemy anymore. God will always be there for me <u>if</u> I make the right choices. He even showed me what my continual choice will be: *to live in constant fear of depression and feeling sorry for myself or, moment by moment, live with Him and never fear anything again."*

The key, as Naomi writes, is depending upon the supernatural power and authority that God has given us to choose His will, regardless of our feelings or our circumstances, and realize with confidence, that no matter what occurs in our lives, He *is* still in control.

## Our Will and The Power to Perform It

What good is knowing we must choose to follow God regardless of our feelings, *if we don't know that God has given us the supernatural willpower*—His authority and His power—*to do so*?

Thus, the most critical area of all our makeup is the new supernatural willpower that we receive as a result of being *born again*. This is our volition or our resolve: it's our will and the power to perform our will. The Greek word for this area is *dianoia*.

Our new willpower has two distinct parts. First, we have God's supernatural will and power given to us as a part of our new birth. This is where God counsels us as to what His will is and gives us the authority to choose it. It's also where He gives us the supernatural power to perform that will in our lives. (Philippians 2:13)

The second part of our willpower, however, is something I wish God had simply left out of my makeup. This is the area we have been talking so much about: *our own free choice*. Our free choice gives us the freedom to either say, "Not my will, but Thine" and then, choose to follow what God has shown us and trust in His ability to perform it in our lives. Or, the free choice to follow what we think, feel and desire, and then trust in our own ability and power to perform that choice in our life.

Over and over again in Scripture, we see the wonderful, and, yet, terrible consequences of man's free will enabling him to either follow *God* or follow *self*. David tearfully humbles himself at the feet of God (Psalm 51), but Saul proudly plots to get his own way (1 Samuel 15). Joseph continually turns away from Potiphar's wife (Genesis 39:7-9), but Samson rushes into the arms of Delilah (Judges 16).

At the exact moment John the Beloved is choosing to lay his head upon Jesus' breast, Judas is choosing to betray Him (John 13:23-27). Mary of Bethany spends a year's income to anoint Jesus with costly perfume (Mark 14:3-9), yet Ananias and Sapphira lie in order to withhold a small portion of their income

(Acts 5:1-11). A poor widow gives her last few coins to the Lord (Luke 21:2-4), but the rich young ruler won't let go of his great wealth (Luke 18:18-25). Parthian magistrates travel a great distance to worship the babe in a manger (Luke 2:1-2), but the Pharisees won't walk six miles into Bethlehem to meet their Messiah!

As Christians, God has given us incredible freedom, moment by moment, to either follow His Spirit and believe and trust in Him, or to follow the flesh and believe and trust in ourselves. He has given us the authority to open ourselves up to Him and abandon ourselves to His will; or, the authority to shut ourselves off from Him and follow what *we* think, feel and desire.

## An Example: Wendy

The following is a wonderful example that illustrates the power of our choices.

A friend of mine, Wendy, had to travel on business from Durango, Colorado to the next town which was 40 miles away. This part of Colorado is spectacularly beautiful, but quite desolate as far as cities or population. There is nothing between Durango and the next town.

Wendy had received *The Way of Agape* audio tapes a few months previously and had been periodically listening to them. She thought this long drive would be a perfect opportunity to finish the series, so she took them along with her. As she became so engrossed in what she was hearing on the tapes (all about our constant, moment-by-moment "faith" choices), she didn't realize she was nearly out of gas and that she had just driven past the last gas station in Durango. There would not be another station for 40 miles.

Sure enough, about 15 or 20 miles outside of Durango, she ran out of gas. The car literally stopped. She pulled over to the side of the road and became totally distraught as she realized her precarious predicament. Since she was going to a business appointment, she was all dressed up (heels and all), thus there was no way she could walk any distance. And even if she could have, there was no place to go for help. The few cars that <u>did</u> pass her, she said, terrified her. They were mostly men with beards and long hair, driving 4x4 trucks with shotguns racked in their rear windows. (Sounds like our cars and trucks in Idaho.)

As she sat there contemplating her situation, God impressed upon her heart what she had been listening to on those tapes—about making faith choices (non-feeling choices), to give any and all situations over to God. It became apparent to her that even in this scary situation, she had a choice. She could either become paralyzed with fear (which she was already beginning to experience) and make *emotional choices* to follow the flesh; or she could make *faith choices*, to relinquish herself to God and trust Him to perform His perfect Will through her (just like she was hearing on the tapes).

She decided to try the latter. Without "feeling" anything, she chose by faith to give God her fear and apprehension and to trust Him to protect her and make a way for her. After her prayer, she decided to try the ignition one more time. She gently turned it on and, surprisingly, the motor sputtered and then started. She was ecstatic! She put the car into first gear and crept down the highway on the far right side. The farther she went, the more elated she became. She had made the appropriate faith choices, God had heard her prayers, and He was now performing a miracle right before her eyes.

Wendy drove that "empty" car all the way (about 20 miles) to the next city. She told me later that when she would come to a hill, she simply made more faith choices to commit herself to God, softly stepped on the gas pedal, and there always seemed to be just enough "oomph" to make it over the hill.

When she finally did arrive at the next city, she stopped at the first gas station feeling absolutely overjoyed. The gas station attendant even asked her if she was all right, because she looked so radiant. She was able to witness to him and tell him the whole story.

Wendy made it to her appointment a little late, but nevertheless, she arrived safely and learned an incredible lesson about God's faithfulness. Now, I don't recommend putting God to the test and going out of town without gas. But, to me, this is a perfect example of the importance of faith choices in our lives. When we trust God enough to constantly choose His way, we free Him to perform miracles. When we don't, we quench His working in our lives.

## God Also Has Two Kinds of Will

What makes all of this so fascinating is that God also has two different kinds of will. In the Greek they are called *thelo*, which means His instinctive, emotional desires (or that which He takes pleasure in); and *boule*, which means His planned purposes (or the resolve of His Mind). Now, of course, for God, both of these kinds of will are "perfect."

Since we are created in the image of God, we, too, have two kinds of will. But, unlike God, what we desire and what we want is not always perfect! The Greek words for these two kinds of "human" will are, *thelema*, which means our own natural, emotional desires (things we take pleasure in); and *boulomai*, which means our "disciplined willing," or our choices free of any emotion (where we depend totally upon God's supernatural will and power within us).

What this says is, we can either make an emotional choice (*thelema*) and be carried away on the tide of emotion by our own uncontrolled feelings, negative thoughts, and self-centered desires (just like an unbeliever); or we can make a faith choice (*boulomai*), a disciplined choice, free of any feelings (but often *against the tide* of our own strong, self-centered emotions) to follow what God has prompted us to do, and then rely upon His strength to perform those choices in our lives.

We must remember that our emotional choices, because they are felt and because they are experienced, are often much stronger in intensity than our faith choices. In other words, emotional choices are ones that we "want" to follow and we "want" to act upon. Remember Debbie in the previous chapter: she was deeply in love with Richard and *she wanted* with all her heart to marry him. Thus, choosing to put her real feelings and emotions aside and make the faith choice she did was extremely difficult. Also, remember Anna in the first chapter, who chose to stay with her adulterous husband even though her own emotions were screaming just the opposite.

Thus, it's important to continually remind ourselves that, yes, *faith choices* are difficult to make and, yes, they go against every natural "feeling" that is in us, but if we succumb to making an emotional choice, we will open ourselves up to the clutches of Satan and be in total bondage to our flesh.

Faith choices—even though they are more difficult to make than emotional choices—are the only choices that free us from the enemy and unleash all of God's power to come to our aid. Consequently, Christians are the only truly free people (if they so choose to be)—free from themselves, free from other's responses, free from their circumstances and Satan's control! This is what Calvary was all about!

As 2 Corinthians 3:17 states, "Where the Spirit of the Lord is, there is liberty [freedom]." That freedom comes in the form of a constant choice!

Again, unbelievers don't have this free choice decision because, again, they don't have another power source within them to perform anything different than what they naturally think, feel and desire. Thus, they are forced to go "with the tide" of emotions.

## Our Willpower—The Passageway of Life

Our willpower, then, is what enables us to put God's Life out into our lives (souls), even when we don't feel like it. It's the passageway, the doorway or the gateway for God's Life (in our hearts) to flow out into our lives. This passageway or doorway can be "opened," so God's Life can flow easily; or it can be "closed," and God's Life will be quenched and blocked.

Remember, we said that our willpower is called, in the Greek, *dianoia*. Well, it's interesting because, *dia* means channel and *noya* means of the mind. And this is exactly what our willpower is, the channel or conduit for God's Spirit to flow from our hearts out into our lives.

Our willpower is the key to whose life will be lived in our soul. Faith choices allow God's Life to come forth; emotional choices quench God's Life. It all comes down to our own choice: Are you willing to set aside what you think, feel and want to do what God asks? Or will you yield to your own self-centered thoughts and emotions and do what you want?

## An Example: "Imagine How You Would Feel!"

Here's a great example.

A young Christian woman wrote to tell me how much she had looked forward to her church's first women's retreat. She was so excited that she had counted the days till the actual weekend arrived. Finally the day came, and for the first 24 hours she said she had a magnificent time. But Saturday night changed everything! There was an "afterglow" service (a time where everyone comes together to seek the Lord). During the worship time, she was moved by the Lord to speak forth what He was telling her, and she opened her mouth and spoke a few words in tongues (a spiritual language that is a gift from God).

No one said a thing to her that night, but the next morning, she overheard the pastor's wife telling one of the new believers that the incident the night before (the speaking in tongues) was "a wasted gift because it was used wrongly." In other words, there was no interpretation of it.

Well, you can imagine the hurt and humiliation my friend felt. She ran outside crying. "Lord, forgive me if I used my gift wrongly." Then, she begged Him to confirm if He truly had told her to speak or not. "Was it from Your Spirit or my flesh?"

Adding further salt to her wound, that evening the pastor's wife again got up in front of the *whole* group and shared, "It was a wasted gift because it was used wrongly—there was no interpretation."

Again, my friend's heart sank. (Just imagine how you would feel if that happened to you.)

Just then a woman from the audience stood up and said, "Oh no, what was spoken last night was definitely from the Lord. He gave me the interpretation, but I was too afraid to speak it out." Then, another lady from the back of the auditorium stood up and she too, said, "I was given the interpretation also, but because I am from another body of believers, I didn't say anything." She spoke what she believed the interpretation was and the first woman said, "Yes, that's exactly what I got also."

My friend started to sob because God was specifically answering her prayer—He was confirming that He *had*, indeed, prompted her to speak. This precious young woman, however, didn't stop there. She made a faith choice to set aside her "justified" hurt and anger, humble herself and go up to the pastor's wife, hug her and tell her that she loved her.

She closed her letter to me by saying, "Nancy, what was so incredible was that I really felt God's Love for this lady. Isn't it an absolute miracle!"

The only route to humility is the Cross. *We are humble only to the extent that we lose ourselves in Him.* This young woman certainly is an example of this.

## Only in Dying Can We Really Live

Thus, the war between our flesh and our spirit is actually waged in our willpower. In other words, our spiritual nature cannot be centered in God without a violent contradiction of our old nature. And this occurs every time we choose by faith. Our flesh, even after we are born again, Spirit-filled and in love with Jesus, is unconvertible, incurable and incorrigible. We cannot change it, fix it or improve it; we must simply surrender it, set it aside and put it to death.

A young woman called not too long ago and shared that she was so discouraged because of the seeming lack of progress in her Christian walk. She thought that the longer she was a Christian, the less self-centered she would become. But, she said, it just wasn't happening that way. In other words, she thought with time she could "improve her self life."

I told her to move over, that she was just like the rest of us. Whether we have been a Christian one year or 51 years, *our self life will never improve with age*! It's still just as ugly and just as self-centered now as it was the first day we believed. We can't tame it, we must continually kill it (crucify it or annihilate it).

Death (the death of our self-life) is the only gateway to real Life! Only dying (choosing to set aside our "self") produces fruit (God's Life). Remember John 12:24, "Unless a corn of wheat falls into the ground and dies, it abideth alone: *but, if it dies, it will bring forth much fruit.*" Thus, God's way of deliverance is only through death. Jesus gave up His own Self for us, and this is His will for us also. We must continually "put off" our old self and "put on" Christ's new one.

Thus, the mature Christian is simply one that recognizes his self life and makes the appropriate choices to give it over to God. "Maturity in Christ" is not knowing an abundance of theological facts, going to church regularly, teaching Bible studies or even writing books, but simply making the right faith choices to cleanse ourselves of all that God shows us, so that His Life can come forth. In other words, the people who are mature are the ones who are constantly watching for and recognizing their own sin. They are mature *only* because they know how to make choices to give themselves over to God.

The way you can tell how mature in the Lord you are, is by how sensitive you are to seeing your own "sin." And it's true: the more mature I become in the Lord, the more sin and self I see in me.

## Our Willpower and The Spirit of Counsel

We have talked extensively about our "free choice," now let's discuss a little more about how God counsels us as to what His will is. So many Christians seem to stumble in this area. How can we really know what God's individual will is for our lives?

Isaiah 11:2 gives us the answer. In this passage, God lists the functions of the seven-fold Spirit of God. One of these functions is called the *Spirit of Counsel.* The Spirit of Counsel means supernatural knowledge of God's will for our own individual lives. In other words, it's God's personal instructions, His directions, to help us make godly choices! (Ephesians 1:11c)

The Spirit of Counsel is like our personal advisor, our helper, our guide. He tells us what we should and shouldn't do. Remember Philippians 2:13, where God promises us that He is in us "...*to will* of His good pleasure." This means God is in us to let us know what His will is for our own particular situation.

The Old Testament word for counsel is *esa* and it means *steerage* or *not letting us veer off course* (i.e., not letting us miss the *mark*—the mark being conformation to His Image). Naturally, only God can keep us straight *on course*, because only He knows our *true* course.

## "Lean Not To Thine Own Understanding"

Years ago, we knew a precious Christian family who lived down the street from us in Newport Beach, California. Their son was critically injured in a diving accident, similar to Joni Erickson Tada, who broke her back and was paralyzed from the neck down. He, too, broke his back and was paralyzed.

The first week after an accident like this is always very critical. Many life-and-death decisions must be made. All the doctors had advised the family that if they wanted their son to survive, he must have a bone fusion operation immediately. This operation was going to be very dangerous, especially because of the boy's already-precarious physical condition.

All the doctors had concurred that the operation was the best course of action and everything had been done to prepare for it. The mom decided to go and be alone with God, pray and seek His Counsel. She told God that she didn't have the slightest clue as to what the best course of action was for her son. But, she acknowledged that God was in control of their lives and she asked Him that if this operation was the wrong decision, that He would intervene.

Proverbs 3:5-6 states, "Trust in the Lord with all thine heart; and lean not unto thine own understanding. In all thy ways acknowledge Him, and He shall direct thy paths."

Just as the boy was about ready to be wheeled into the operating room, an uncle who was also a neurosurgeon on the East Coast called and told the family definitely <u>not</u> to have the operation. I've forgotten all the medical reasons he gave them, but the family felt God was intervening, so they chose to postpone the operation.

I'm sure the doctors were completely baffled at the family's decision, but they nevertheless conceded. Less than two hours after that phone call, the son came down with a serious respiratory problem and had he been in the middle of that operation, he never would have survived.

That operation was scheduled three more times. But in each case, God supernaturally intervened and managed to stop it. One time while the son was receiving a transfusion in preparation for the operation, he developed an allergic reaction and burst out with hives. Once again, the operation was postponed.

The last I heard, the boy never had that operation, but had survived the ordeal and was doing quite well.

## Our Willpower and The Spirit of Strength

Going hand in hand with God's supernatural Counsel, is God's Spirit of Strength, again listed in Isaiah 11:2 as part of the seven-fold Spirit of God.

God's Spirit of Strength is God's supernatural ability to take what He has counseled us, bring it forth, and then perform it or accomplish it in our lives. In other words, what good is knowing what God's will is if we don't have the strength or the power to carry it out?

Again, Philippians 2:13 tells us, "For it is God which worketh in you, both *to will* [counseling us as to what His Will is] and *to do* [giving us His Power and ability to perform that Will in our lives]..."

God doesn't need any of our own natural abilities or strengths in order to help Him accomplish His will. In fact, when we try to perform His will in our own strength, we simply get in the way. Even though we might have great capabilities and assets of our own, we must still choose to set those aside and trust Him in everything. He tells us, "Without Me, ye can do nothing." (John 15:5) In other words, everything we do in our own ability, apart from His Spirit of Strength, is going to chalk up to worthlessness.

## Self-Confidence Didn't Help A Bit!

Years ago, I went to teach a class while feeling particularly confident about myself. God had given me the material I needed for the class, I was excited about it and I felt *confident* (always a warning signal) that I could present it well. I really "felt" up (woops, emotions, watch out!) for speaking that day.

When I got up to the podium, however, I recognized that *I* was the one doing the performing and not God! My *self-confidence* and *self-assurance* had quenched His Spirit and I was definitely "in the flesh." I panicked and wanted to run because I know how we can "bomb" when we perform in our own strength. Consequently, the whole time I was teaching, I was frantically going through the steps of giving my pride over to God.

My dressing well, my being put together emotionally and mentally and my knowing the material well, didn't help a bit. God must still be *the One* we rely totally upon.

As Scripture says, "I can do all things [only] through Christ who strengthens me." (Philippians 4:13) Thus, all self-confidence must be confessed and replaced with God-confidence; all self-esteem (*I like what I do* and what I am) must also be set aside and replaced with God-esteem (*I like what God does through me* and what He makes of me); and all self-reliance must be superseded by God's strength and His ability. In other words, it's not what *we* can do for God, but *what God will do through us*.

This is why it's critical that God does both the *counseling* and the *performing* of His will. If God does both, then He will be the one who will get the glory. As Jeremiah 9:23-24 declares, "Thus saith the Lord, Let not the wise man glory in his wisdom, neither let the mighty man glory in his might, let not the rich man glory in his riches: but let him that glorieth glory in this, that he understandeth and knoweth Me, that I am the Lord which exercise loving-kindness, judgment and righteousness, in the earth: for in these things I delight, saith the Lord."

## Spirit-Control

God's Spirit of Strength in the Greek means *power to rein in*, mastery over self, self-control, or better yet, *Spirit-control*. This is exactly what God's Spirit of Strength does. It reins in (or brings into captivity) our self-life, so that God's Life can come forth. Luke 21:19 even says, "In your patience possess [or rein in] your souls."

When we are going through troubled times and we make faith choices not to go by what we feel, think or want, but to go God's way, God will then give us His supernatural Strength to set aside our wild feelings, uncontrolled thoughts and self-centered desires so that we can act out of His Spirit and His Life.

God's Spirit of Counsel and Strength are simply God's authority and God's Power to *put off* the habits of the flesh and to *put on* Christ.

## An Example: "She Just Glowed"

Here's an example of how one woman not only chose to follow God's counsel, but also how she laid down her life so that God's Spirit of strength could perform His will through her.

Karla grew up in a Christ-centered, Spirit-filled home, married her high school sweetheart and moved to Virginia to work at CBN (Christian Broadcasting Network). She and her husband, Jim, got along wonderfully until about five years into their marriage when she became pregnant. Jim was in the Navy and scheduled to go out to sea shortly, therefore, he would miss the birth of their child. Karla was very upset and as she began to cling to him for support and love, their marriage deteriorated rapidly. Jim just emotionally pulled away and thus, she felt abandoned long before his ship ever actually left the dock.

Once Jim left, Karla went downhill quickly and became seriously depressed. Her doctor sent her to a psychiatrist, but he couldn't seem to help her. She prayed and prayed, but got no direction. When Jim returned after about six months, Karla, once again, began to stranglehold him to meet her needs. This time their marriage really hit bottom. Jim simply shut her out of his life.

During this difficult time, Karla got a new job at CBN and began working with a department secretary that she had previously known. Karla remembered this woman as always being very quiet and sort of sad, but now *she just glowed* all the time. Karla thought to herself, "What's going on? Why is she so doggoned happy?"

Finally, Karla had a chance to talk with her and asked her point blank, "Why are you so different? What has happened? How come you are always so happy?" Her friend shared about her own painful marriage and how awful it had been, but how God had miraculously healed it. She told Karla that the natural love in her marriage had absolutely evaporated, but God had given her the supernatural Love she needed to initiate love to her husband "right where he was." As she learned to genuinely give her complaints over to the Lord and become an open vessel, God was able to love her husband through her. She suggested that Karla might want to try this way of *Agape*, because she had found that God was the only One who could heal her heart, the only One who could meet her needs and the only One who could be the Lover of her soul.

Deep down inside, Karla knew that she was selfish, even after all her whining, complaining and screaming. She also knew that much of the problem in their marriage was of her own making. She began to put into practice what her friend had suggested. At first she cried oceans of tears, but the more she tried giving herself over to the Lord, the more she knew she wanted this changed life. As she learned how to make more and more faith choices—non-feeling choices—to follow God, regardless of how she felt and what she thought, she found it worked! At times, however, she admitted that real death seemed preferable to another death of her own will!

Slowly, Karla began to fall in love with Jesus all over again and He began to heal her heart. When she spoke to Jim, she could sense there wasn't any more "venom" coming forth: instead, God's peace literally wrapped around her like a blanket. As she trusted God to change her thoughts and emotions, and give her the Love and wisdom she needed, her marriage began to slowly improve.

Karla closes her letter by saying, "Our marriage is now NOTHING like it was before. We talk, we laugh and I enjoy my husband's company and want to be with him all the time. After 14 years of being in the Navy, Jim is getting out *because he doesn't want to leave me or go back to sea.* Nancy, can you believe it?"

Now, Karla is the one who is glowing!

------------------------------

God's principles *do* work, regardless of our circumstances. Whether we are talking marriage relationships, business relationships, family relationships or friends and acquaintances, if we choose to die to our own will and desires, God can accomplish His perfect will through us.

Walking in God's counsel and His strength is the victory that overcomes the world. This is what faith is all about. (1 John 5:4) Again, faith is simply a series of choices—choices not only allowing Him to work, but also choices giving Him our lives to work through. Overcomers are those who prevail over what their own thoughts, emotions, and desires are urging them to do, in order to allow God's Spirit to control them instead.

This is the *preparation* (the equipping, the cleansing) that each of us must choose to do daily. It's our own responsibility to *put off* the old and to *put on* the new. (Ephesians 4:22-24) We already possess Christ's Life in our hearts; our job is simply to make sure that's the Life that is showing forth in our souls. This is what will gird us for the battle ahead. (Ephesians 6:10)

## Not Only a Faith Choice, But a Faith Walk

Consequently, it's not only important that we make the right faith choices, giving God the authority to work, but it's also important that we give Him our lives to perform those choices through. In other words, we must continually "present [our] bodies as a living sacrifice, holy, acceptable unto God, which is [our] reasonable service...that [we] might prove [by our life actions] what is that good, and acceptable, and perfect, will of God." (Romans 12:1-2)

How often we make the right choices in our prayer closets, giving God the authority to work. But, because we don't feel any different when we begin to walk, act and do what He asked, we doubt that we really heard Him and, once again, we take our lives back into our control. What makes giving Him our lives such a difficult step is that we often "feel" one way, and yet, by faith we must choose to "act" in another way. For example: how much easier it is for a wife of an alcoholic to make the right choices to follow God *in the privacy of her own prayer closet*, than it is for her to surrender her life to the Lord when she *actually encounters her verbally abusive husband.* In this case, she must not only trust God to take away her natural feelings of anger, bitterness and resentment and show her what His will is, but she must also trust Him enough to give her the Love, wisdom and power she needs to walk that will out.

Getting up and *doing in action* what God has asked us to do, is saying like Peter, "At Thy word I will." (Luke 5:5) In other words, we are trusting that God will perform His Will and His Life through us, regardless of how we feel.

If this is a difficult step, I would suggest reading Philippians 2:5-9. This is the passage that talks about being "obedient unto death," not only on the inside—choosing to lay aside our own thoughts and emotions—but also, on the outside—getting up and actually doing in action whatever God has called us to do.

## A Classic Example:  I Almost Drowned

Many years ago, Chuck and I went to Australia on a business trip. We decided to celebrate our anniversary early by going to the Great Barrier Reef to do some scuba diving. Chuck has always loved to dive, and one of his greatest desires was to someday dive at the Great Barrier Reef. This was a perfect opportunity.

I, however, had not made a dive in 10 years. Ten years previously, I had taken a one-week scuba "crash course" so I could get certified and go diving with Chuck in the Virgin Islands. We had a great time, but

I hadn't had the opportunity to dive since then. So I had not thought about diving—or even tried out the equipment—in 10 years! I was so busy traveling and writing before this trip that I didn't even have time to reread the diving manual.

Arriving at Hayman Island on the Great Barrier Reef very late in the afternoon, we immediately asked if there were any "refresher courses" offered before the big dive the next morning. They said "no." Then we asked if there was a possibility of an afternoon boat trip the next day so I could take the morning practice course. Again, the answer was "no."

They also told us if we wanted to go on the planned trip to the Reef early the next morning, we needed to take a quick "check out" dive right then. They needed to see if we were proficient. (Oh boy, just what I was afraid of!) Well, Chuck passed with flying colors.

I jumped into the water ready to do my very best. The instructor made me sit on the bottom of the pool, take off my breathing apparatus and my mask, and put them both back on. Well, after 10 years, I had forgotten exactly how to do this properly. I couldn't remember how to "clear" my mask underwater. I could only clear the water down to just above my nose. After one minute of holding my breath, I finally had to breathe in. Tons of water went into my lungs. Instinctively, I shot to the top. (A cardinal rule in diving is that you never shoot to the top. You can easily kill yourself by holding your breath while going up—causing an embolism. A change in depth of only three feet can prove fatal.)

The instructor followed me to the top, calmed me down, and said everything would be okay and to try again. He then led me back underwater to try out the "buddy breathing" technique. At the bottom of the pool, he took a deep breath and then handed me his breathing apparatus. Again, I had forgotten you don't just breathe in when you put the apparatus in your mouth. You must first blow out through the regulator to get rid of the water that has come in as it was passed to you. I took a deep breath, expecting to get air, but got a mouthful of water instead. Once again, I instinctively shot to the top.

The instructor was very nice, and surprisingly said I could go on the trip the next morning, but he said he was a "little nervous" for me. He was nervous? At this point I was panic stricken! I had almost killed myself twice in only eight feet of water; what would I do the next morning in 100 feet of water?

All night long, fear absolutely gripped me! I'm not normally prone to be fearful, but that night I was paralyzed! I made up my mind: there was no way I was going on that boat trip the next morning. The problem was, however, it was Chuck's birthday, and he had his heart set on diving at the Barrier Reef, and he had told me that he wouldn't go without me. What on earth was I supposed to do?

I didn't sleep half the night. I just lied there awake. By faith (because I certainly didn't feel it), I kept giving God my fear and panic, telling Him that I was willing to trust Him with whatever He wanted me to do. I acknowledged it was His body and His life (He owns me), and I committed to rely on Him totally. I finally fell asleep and when I woke the next morning, I knew in my heart that God would not fail me.

Chuck and I didn't talk much about the diving trip at breakfast, because I'm sure he sensed my fear and that I might say, "I'm not going."

After breakfast we took a walk and "coincidently" ran across a gal whom we had befriended on the boat coming to the Island the day before. She mentioned that she was taking a scuba diving refresher course that morning and then was going on an afternoon boat trip to the Reef. She asked us if we would like to accompany her and her husband. Well, we were floored because of the response we had gotten from the diving people the night before that there was no morning refresher course and no afternoon boat trip.

I knew immediately it had to be the Lord! He knew how badly I needed that refresher course and He had arranged one just for me!

I took the diving course with my new friend and we went on that afternoon boat trip. I made several dives with my precious husband and we had an absolute ball, taking loads of pictures and even seeing several sharks.

This is just one small example, but these "little hassles" are where we often live. If God can be trusted in these tiny tests, how much more can He be trusted in the big ones? Trusting God is simply relying upon Him and His ability to accomplish His will in our lives, no matter how we feel, what we think, or what our circumstances are. We can't serve God with our words only; we must also put our life actions alongside.

As Habakkuk 2:4 states, "The just shall live by His faith." In other words, we live the life that pleases Christ by trusting His faithfulness to perform that life in and through us.

## How Much Do You Trust God?

The bottom line: *How much do you trust God?*

We often sing about His Love and His mercy, but do we really believe in it? A child trusts in the love of his mother, even though, at times, she must discipline him and take him to the doctor for shots. Real love involves trust. *When someone really loves and cares for you, you trust that they have your best interests at heart, even though you don't always understand their expression of love.* God asks us to do the same with Him. He asks us to unconditionally trust in His Love for us, no matter what we see, feel or understand to be happening.

The God of the Bible is a loving and compassionate Father, who will use all the events in our lives to rid us of *sin* and *self*, so that He might replace us with Himself and, thereby, fill us with His fullness. He continually stretches and shapes our faith so that we will be able to endure any circumstance that

He allows, and so that we will be able to say with absolute conviction, "Though [You] slay me, yet will I trust [You]." (Job 13:15) *This is the kind of faith that overcomes the world, and this is the kind of faith that brings with it a peace that passes all understanding.*

How much do you trust Him? Enough to lay everything down?

# Chapter Four
## Single-minded vs. Double-minded

Maggie found out that her husband, Mark, was having an affair. She was devastated and not quite sure which way to turn. Mark began to come home only for a few days at a time, and then he would leave again for weeks. At the same time, he also began to drink heavily and smoke "pot."

Mark had had a very troubled youth and was raised in a "gang-type" environment. He was involved with people who committed terrible crimes and who had consistently abused drugs. Maggie knew about Mark's background when they first began dating, but she had fallen in love with the tender, beautiful man inside and thought she could be instrumental in changing his life.

Shortly after they married, however, he began doing heroin. He was arrested and sentenced to five years in prison. While incarcerated, he became "on fire" for the Lord and was released early because of his good behavior. Maggie thought all the bad times were finally behind them. She became pregnant, had two beautiful daughters and life became bliss. After several years, however, Mark began to again stray. Maggie felt it was her job as his wife to keep him "straight," so she put up all sorts of rules and conditions. But, of course, this only made Mark hate being home. He lost his job and began to live off of their credit cards.

When Maggie finally found out about the other woman, she came to the conclusion "enough is enough" and decided to leave. She got a legal separation and a restraining order against Mark, so that he couldn't harass her or "come by anytime he wanted." Not being able to see his wife or his girls devastated Mark. And when he realized that Maggie was really going to divorce him, he totally broke. This was the first step towards repentance.

Five and a half months after Mark's affair was over, Maggie returned to the marriage. She felt strongly that the Lord had told her to come home. She chose to trust God totally, by faith, unconditionally forgive Mark and become willing to start over again. She really did love Mark and, more than anything else, wanted to rebuild their marriage.

It hasn't been easy for Maggie, but she writes, "How awesome it's been since I have chosen, on a daily basis, to be a cleansed vessel and present my body to God as a living sacrifice. *The realization that I can make a choice to do what God wants me to do, even when I don't feel like it, has helped me tremendously. I didn't know you didn't have to "feel willing," but simply "be willing." I am happy to say that it really works!*

## Our Mind: A Whole Conceptual Process

In the first chapter, we noted that our thoughts are what stir up our emotions; our emotions then influence our choices; and our choices are what produce our lives. This is why our *thinking* is so very important to

God and why He puts such emphasis on our thoughts throughout the Bible. 2 Corinthians 10:5 tells us to, "Take every thought captive" and then, deal with the ones that are not of faith. Thus, *the battle for our lives is really waged in our thinking.* In other words, whoever controls our minds will ultimately be the one who controls our lives. In this chapter, we want to *visually* see how this works and why our choices are so very critical.

Let's begin by exploring how the Bible defines our minds and see if we can understand a little more clearly why the Lord considers our minds so important. According to Scripture, *our minds are not just our thoughts or our reason or our intellect, but a whole conceptual process.* This process begins with the spirit that resides at the core of our being and ends with the life that is produced out in our soul. This whole process is called "mind," or *nous,* in the Greek. (Romans 12:2)

CHART 1 on the next page is a visual picture of how this conceptual process works.

As you look at this chart, you can see that the spirit, which is the power source or the energy source of our lives, creates the thoughts of our hearts. And then those thoughts are produced out in our lives (or, our souls) as actions. In other words, the spirit creates the thoughts of our hearts and those thoughts then produce our life actions. This whole process, according to the Bible, is called our mind.

# What is our Mind?

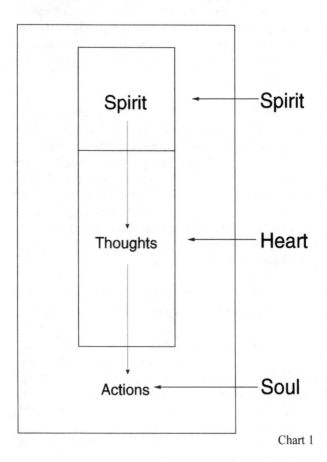

Chart 1

## Three Types of Minds

Scripture speaks about three types of minds: *the natural mind (an unbeliever), a double-minded person (a Christian) and a single-minded person (also a Christian).*

See CHART 2 on next page.

"Mind" in the natural man, i.e. an unbeliever, one who has no influence from God, is going to be a natural, self-centered conceptual process. This natural process begins with his human spirit, residing at the core of his being, creating self-centered thoughts in his heart and, eventually, self-centered life actions in his soul.

For this unbelieving person, there is no other choice because there is no other spirit, no other power source, or no other life source within him to produce something different than what his own human spirit is prompting him to think and do. (1 Corinthians 2:14)

Turn to CHART 3 on following page.

"Mind" in a believer, someone who has asked Jesus Christ into his heart, however, *should be* a God-centered conceptual process, because God's Spirit dwells at the core of his being. In other words, God's Spirit is the One who creates God-centered thoughts in this person's heart, which *should then* produce God-centered life actions in his soul. This is God's perfect will and His ideal design.

# Unbeliever's Mind

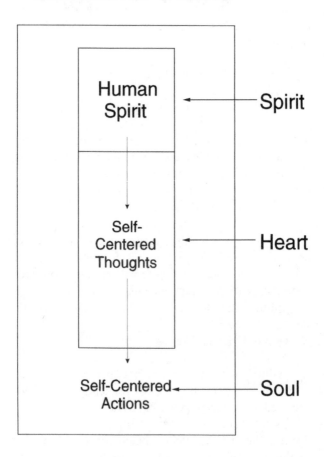

Chart 2

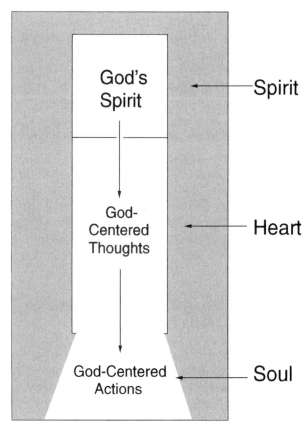

Single-mindedness

Chart 3

This God-centered conceptual process is called in Scripture "single-mindedness." It means *one-souled*, because there is only one life being lived here— God's. In other words, God's Life is freely coming forth from this person's heart and producing godly life actions in his soul. This is a person who, for the moment, has been conformed into Christ's image and is living the truth.

## A Perfect Example: Joseph

A Scriptural example of someone who is single-minded would be Joseph in Genesis 39. As you may recall, after Joseph was sold to the Ishmaelites traveling to Egypt, he was assigned to work in the household of Potiphar, an officer of Pharaoh and captain of the guard. Potiphar chose Joseph to be an overseer of his house because he trusted him completely. Potiphar committed everything into Joseph's hands and God blessed Potiphar because of this.

Potiphar's wife, however, was not as trustworthy. When Potiphar was gone, she enticed Joseph to lay with her. Refusing her offer, Joseph responded with, "How could I do that to Potiphar when he has entrusted everything to me? And besides, how could I sin against God?" Potiphar's wife wouldn't take no for an answer and, day after day, kept persisting.

One day, when Joseph went into the house, she physically caught hold of him. As he tried to flee, she ripped off his garment and kept it as evidence against him. She lied to the servants and to her husband that evening by saying that Joseph had attacked her. Potiphar was grieved, but he had no other choice but to put Joseph in prison.

The Lord adds a footnote to this story in Genesis 39:21. He says, "But the Lord was with Joseph, and showed him mercy and gave him favor..." It also goes on to say that all who saw Joseph knew God was with him.

Joseph, to me, is a perfect example of a person who is single-minded. Even though he was repeatedly tempted, he kept on *choosing* to give God his own thoughts so that God's Life could still freely come forth.

Because of his *choice* to stay single-minded, Joseph was conformed to God's image and everyone was aware that God was with him. In other words, he showed forth *His* character.

Unfortunately, there is another choice for a Christian, and this is where many of us live our entire Christian lives.

See CHART 4 on the next page.

This is a picture of a believer who has God's Thoughts in his heart (he's a Christian), but because he has chosen to follow his own lusts, hurts, frustration, anger (justified or not), etc., God's Life has been blocked from coming forth and in it's place, self-centered life actions are produced.

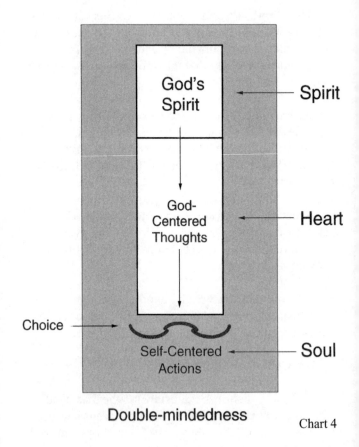

**Double-mindedness**

Chart 4

This is called double-mindedness, or being "twice-souled." It means that two lives are being lived—God's and his own. This then, is a Christian who is *being conformed to the world's image*, not Christ's.

Consequently, we can be Christians all of our lives with God's Life in our hearts, and yet because we continue to make *emotional choices* to follow what <u>we</u> think, feel and desire over what God has prompted us to do (deny self, pick up our cross and follow Him), God's Life in us is quenched. Thus, no one will ever see the difference between our life and that of our neighbors who don't even know God. Yes, we're Christians, but ones who are living *two* lives. God's supernatural Life is still in our hearts, but the life that is coming forth from our soul is "self life," our own thoughts and emotions, and not God's at all.

Double-mindedness is what a "carnal" Christian fights continuously. He still has God's Spirit energizing God's new supernatural Life in his heart, but he has chosen to hang onto his own self-centered thoughts, emotions, and desires, thereby quenching God's Life in him and showing forth his own "self life" (the old man) instead. Double-mindedness, then, is what makes us hypocrites or phonies.

Titus 1:16 describes this state, "They profess that they know God [intimately], but in works [actions] they deny Him..."

Double-mindedness, obviously, is the enemy's game plan. He knows that double-mindedness will immediately quench God's Life in us and thus, the Gospel will not be passed on. Therefore, he will do everything he can to get us to choose to follow what we are thinking and feeling, rather than denying ourselves and following Christ.

The enemy knows that, "...Every kingdom divided against itself is brought to desolation; and a house divided against a house falleth." (Luke 11:17)

## An Example:  David

A perfect Scriptural example of double-mindedness is, again, David in 2 Samuel 11. As you recall, David was on the roof of his palace when he saw Bathsheba bathing next door. He thought she was absolutely beautiful and he wanted her. Rather than catch those first ungodly thoughts as Joseph had, however, David allowed those lustful thoughts to stir up his emotions, feed his desires and finally influence his actions.

David sent his servants to inquire after the woman. They came back and reported that she was Bathsheba, the wife of Uriah. But the thought that she was someone else's wife, however, didn't stop David. He was so emotionally wrapped up by this time that he chose to act upon his own desires, sent for Bathsheba and laid with her. When David learned that Bathsheba was pregnant, he called Uriah home, thinking he could cover his own sin. Uriah, however, in deference to his men on the front lines of the war, didn't sleep with his wife, but rested on the porch of his house.

When David found out that his cover-up had not worked, he commanded that Uriah be put at the front lines of the battle and that the troops be pulled back from him. Just as David had hoped, Uriah was killed. David then took Bathsheba as his wife.

To me, David's behavior presents a perfect example of a double-minded man. Even though he had God's Life in his heart and had been "a man after God's own heart," he nevertheless chose to *go with the tide* and follow the lusts of his own flesh over what God was prompting him to do. (Acts 13:22c)

James 1:14-15 is provocative in light of David's story: "...Every man is tempted, when he is drawn away [from making the right faith choice] by his own lust [a strong desire], and enticed [captured by it]. Then when lust hath conceived [they have made the choice to follow it], it brings forth sin; and sin, when it is finished, brings forth death [separation from God]."

For this short period of time, David lived a lie. His words, "I love God," and his actions obviously did not match. People could no longer see God in him. He totally had given himself over to his own will and desires, and thus, God's Life was quenched.

The Lord adds a footnote to this story and in 2 Samuel 11:27 it says, "...The thing that David had done displeased the Lord," and it also caused "...the enemies of the Lord to blaspheme." (2 Samuel 12:14)

How Satan revels in our double-mindedness!  He knows that double-mindedness not only keeps us bound by our hurts and wounds, but it also, causes the enemies of God to blaspheme.  Thus, all Satan and his hordes want, is to have us respond "emotionally."  Then, he's got us!

Scripture tells us that double-mindedness will: 1) "keep us unstable in all our ways" (James 1:8); 2) quench the "light of the knowledge" of Jesus in our lives (Luke 11:34c); and finally, 3) cause us to fall (Luke 11:17).

## Simplicity in Christ

In 2 Corinthians 11:3 Paul warns us about double-mindedness.  He says, "I fear lest by any means as the serpent beguiled Eve through his subtlety, so your minds should be corrupted from the simplicity that is in Christ!"

*Simplicity* does not mean ignorance, naiveté or being unschooled in the things of God; it simply means "singleness of mind."  The Greek word for simplicity is *haplous*, which can be defined as "something that is folded together, braided together or intertwined."  Simplicity in Christ means having our thinking folded together with and focused on Christ.  *Haplous*, therefore, is the same thing as single-mindedness.

Paul is saying here that just as Satan deceived, seduced and tricked Eve in her thinking, so he fears that our own thinking can easily be corrupted from the simplicity or the single-mindedness that is in Christ.

And he's absolutely right.  Because we have <u>not</u> understood the power and authority that we possess to make faith choices and stay single-minded, we've not been prepared to stand in the battle against Satan, and we've ended up crashing and burning even before we've begun.

## An Example:  "Tired of Trying"

Three years ago, Ginny was facing a possible divorce.  She and her husband, Doug, had come to a brick wall in their relationship.  They were simply exhausted and tired of "trying and trying and trying."  Out of desperation, Ginny began a *Way of Agape* class to learn more about God's Love.  Through this class, Ginny began to see her relationship with Doug through God's eyes.  The deep wounds that they had each brought into their marriage still hindered the kind of married life they both desired.

Slowly, Ginny began to see how hurts from her childhood (and an extremely bad relationship with her father) had made her the person she was.  Her reactions in her marriage were simply a reflection of those buried hurts.  As she began to see those things and make the appropriate choices to give them to God, things began to change drastically.  Doug noticed first and was thrilled; then, all her children saw the change also.

It wasn't easy, but the more Ginny learned about the principles of loving God first (choosing to totally give ourselves over to Him), she and Doug committed to beginning their relationship one more time. They renewed their vows and took their first honeymoon.

She writes that now she and her father have reconciled and that he has, for the first time, expressed his love for her. Doug has been so touched and changed by all that has transpired, he recently recommitted his life to the Lord.

The same state of frustration and exhaustion that Ginny and Doug experienced in their marriage can be seen in the Body of Christ now. Because of our ignorance as to how to make faith choices to do the Lord's will, regardless of how we feel, we have become "pot-shots" for Satan, just like Paul warned. Again, like Ginny and Doug, most of us have not understood that by surrendering ourselves to God, we *can* be "set free" from our fears, hurts, doubts, lusts, memories, unforgiveness and every other negative thought and emotion that quenches His Life in our hearts. Christ not only wants to take these things from us "as far as the east is from the west," He also wants to replace them with His Wisdom, Counsel, Strength and Knowledge.

## The Light of God's Life

God's plan for our lives is that we might be conformed into His image so that we can show forth His Light (His Life), and the Gospel can be passed on.

Luke 11:33-36 perfectly describes both single-mindedness and double-mindedness: "No man, when he hath lighted a candle, putteth it in a secret place, neither under a bushel, but on a candlestick, that they which come in may see the light. The light of the body is the eye: therefore when thine eye is single [single-minded], thy whole body also is full of light; but when thine eye is evil [double-minded], thy body also is full of darkness. Take heed therefore, that the light which is in thee be not darkness [covered over]. If thy whole body therefore be full of light, having no part dark, the whole shall be full of light, as when the bright shining of a candle doth give thee light."

Jesus' Life is the Light that Luke is talking about here (John 8:12), and our goal and purpose as Christians is not only to be filled with that Light, but also to let that Light shine out to others. We are not to hide that light under a bushel (under a wall of hurts, doubts and fears), but, as this Scripture says, put it on a lampstand so *all* can see it. In other words, be a genuine witness of Christ—show forth His Life.

## Which Will It Be: Light or Darkness?

Turn back to CHART 3 and let's see visually how this works.

In the above passage in Luke, it says that when we are single-minded we will have a body full of light. In other words, Jesus' Life will exude from us like a flashlight. It will be on a lampstand where all can see it. Look at CHART 3 and you can see exactly what this might look like. Can you see the flashlight effect? (Luke 12:35)

Now, turn back to CHART 4.

When we are double-minded, even though we are Christians, we'll have a body that is full of darkness, because God's Life in our hearts will have been quenched by "self" (fears, insecurities, unforgiveness, anger, etc.).

This exemplifies what Jesus meant when He talked about His Life—His Light—being under a bushel. We are covering it over with hurts, bitterness, resentments, etc., which then forces us to live our self life, our own thoughts and emotions. This is why we often want to "wear masks and facades." We don't want others to see who we really are and that we're not really walking as we should. (Now, we're not exactly sure "why" we can't walk as we should, because we want to. But we know in our hearts, this is not it!)

This is why so many of us get tired of "trying" to live the Christian life. We're tired of "playing" Christ. We don't understand that the Christian Life is simply recognizing our own sin and self, handing it over to God, and then watching *Him live the Christian Life out through us*.

## God Wants us to be "Spirit-Filled"

Just as Solomon's Temple in 1 Kings 8:10-11 and 2 Chronicles 5:13-14 was filled from the inside out with God's Spirit, this is exactly God's purpose for our lives.

Daily we are to allow God's Spirit to issue forth from the Holy of Holies of our hearts and fill our souls and our bodies with His Life, His Light and His Glory. This is <u>not</u> just a one-time event; it's a moment-by-moment choice to be filled with His Spirit.

"...Be ye not unwise, but understanding what the will of the Lord is. "...[that ye] be [being] filled with the Spirit [all day long, every day]." (Ephesians 5:17-18; John 7:38)

"For ye are bought with a price: therefore glorify [be filled with, reflect, manifest and shine forth] God in your body..." (1 Corinthians 6:20)

## Our Choice

Again, the only way this is ever going to happen— the only way we are ever going to be single-minded or filled with God's Spirit—is by learning how to make faith choices to go God's way, even if it's the last thing in the world we want to do. Learning how to *put off* the garbage in our thinking and *put on* Christ is the only way we can ever reflect Him. Only then, can God's Spirit freely issue forth from the Holy of Holies of our hearts and fill our souls as He desires.

See CHART 5 on the next page.

Thus, it will be our continual choice which way we will choose:

1) We can follow God's will by obeying His Word, trusting His Spirit to perform His Word in our lives, and then doing whatever He asks, thus ending up single-minded and Spirit-filled; <u>or</u>

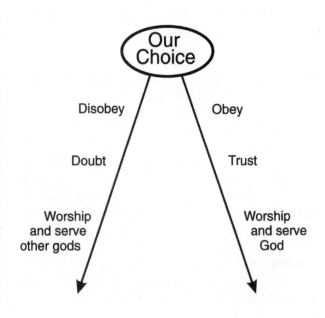

Chart 5

2) We can follow our *own* will by disobeying Him, not trusting Him, and then doing what we want, thus, ending up double-minded and full of self.

Again, it's a mind battle. Whoever controls our thinking will ultimately control our lives. When we don't understand how to make faith choices to surrender ourselves to God, we'll become conformed to the world and the enemy will rejoice. If, however, we can learn to follow Christ even when we don't feel like it, want to or think it will work, we'll have a chance to be conformed into Christ's image and able to stand against the enemy of our souls.

Therefore, our efforts to change should <u>not</u> be focused on our wrong actions, but on our wrong thinking and our wrong choices. Only by constantly "taking every thought captive," putting off the debris and putting on Christ, will we ever be able to walk the victorious Christian life.

## Be Willing

All that God requires for us to live the Christian Life is that we are clean and that we are *willing*. The dictionary defines willing as "ready to act without hesitation."

Luke 14:26 reminds us that we really cannot be God's disciples unless we are "willing to" (not wanting to or feeling like it, but simply *willing to*) lay everything down (father, mother, wife, children, brothers, sisters). "Yea," He says, "[even our] own lives."

Several years ago, while having lunch with some dear old friends, we began to talk about how important it is for us to be willing to deny ourselves, lay everything down to Jesus and follow Him. One friend of mine said, "Nancy, I don't agree with you. I think some people don't have the ability or the capability to lay everything down and do it God's way." She then gave various reasons why she was convinced they couldn't do this: dysfunctional families, co-dependency, poor marriages, physical abuse, emotional problems, and other environmental circumstances.

I thought for a moment and then replied, "Suzy, if these people are Christians, then God is in them. Right?" "Right," she said. "Well, then, *He* is the One who will make them capable and give them the ability to deny themselves. I think *all Christians* are capable of laying themselves aside because God is in them, *but not all Christians are willing to do so*! That, to me, is the bottom line!"

The people Suzy was talking about simply weren't willing to lay themselves aside. Their excuses ranged from "dysfunctional families," to "my husband is not trying." But, I don't believe these things were the *real* problem, because God has all the Love, Wisdom and Power they need; they just weren't willing to set themselves aside so that God could do these things through them.

Perhaps this example will help us to understand Matthew 24:12 a little more clearly. This Scripture says that in the end times "...because iniquity shall abound, the *Agape* of many will grow cold." This is simply saying that in the end times, many Christians will <u>not</u> be willing to deny themselves, but rather want to hold on to their "justified" hurts, unforgiveness, etc. Therefore, the *Agape* Love of God in their hearts *will grow cold.* It will be covered over, blocked and unable to flow forth.

*Thus, the bottom line is that all Christians have God's Love in them, but not all Christians are willing to set themselves aside to let it flow.*

God promises us in Luke 18:30, as well as in many other Scriptures, that the more we are willing to deny ourselves, the more He will return a hundredfold, not only "in this present time" but "in the world to come" as well. I know this has been true in my own life. My first book *Why Should I Be the First to Change?* shares how God has restored a hundredfold my marriage, my family, my kids, etc. because I finally learned how to surrender myself to God. I'm certainly not any more capable than anybody else, but one thing *is* for certain: I'm willing. And that seems to be all that's necessary!

The question is: Are you?

As Matthew 16:24 says, "If any man [is willing to] come after Me, let him *deny himself,* and *take up his cross,* and *follow Me.*"

# Chapter Five
## *Faith Choices*

In the mid-1930s, a German pastor was abducted from his church, handcuffed, taken to prison and immediately put into a five-foot cell. Suspected of aiding Jews, there was no hearing, no trial—not even time to let his family know what had happened to him.

For weeks, this gentle pastor asked the prison guard outside his cell door if he could use the phone at the end of the hall to call his wife and family and, at least, let them know he was alive. The guard, however, was a contemptible man who hated anyone who had to do with Jewry. He not only wouldn't let the pastor use the phone, he also determined in his heart to make the pastor's life as miserable as possible.

The sadistic guard purposefully skipped the pastor's cell when meals were handed out; he made the pastor go weeks without a shower; he kept lights burning in his room so he couldn't sleep; he blasted his shortwave radio hoping the constant noise would break the pastor's spirit; he used filthy language; he pushed him; he shoved him; and, when he could, he arranged for the pastor to have the most difficult job in the labor force.

The pastor, on the other hand, prayed over and over again not to let his natural hate for this guard consume him. He "chose" instead to forgive him and to show him God's unconditional Love. As the months went by, whenever he could, the pastor smiled at the guard; he thanked him when his meals did come; when the guard was near his cell, the pastor told him about his own wife and his children; he even questioned the guard about his own family and about his goals, ideas and visions; and, one time, for a quick moment, he had a chance to tell the guard about Christ and His Love.

The guard never answered a word, but, obviously, heard it all.

After months of choosing to unconditionally love this terrible guard, God's Love finally broke through. One night, as the pastor was again quietly talking to him, the guard cracked a smile. The next day, instead of his cell being skipped for lunch, the pastor got two. The following evening, he was allowed not only to go to the showers, but also to stay as long as he wanted. The lights began going off at night in his cell and the radio noise ceased. Finally, one afternoon, the guard came into the pastor's cell, asked him for his home phone number, and he, personally, made the long-awaited call to the pastor's family.

A few months later the pastor was mysteriously released, with no questions asked.

This is an example of what happens when we use the incredible authority and power of God to make choices we don't feel, but know that God wants us to make. God not only enabled this pastor to make choices by faith, He also changed his feelings to align with those choices. In the natural, the pastor hated this guard and was certainly justified, by worldly standards, in doing so. But he loved Jesus more than himself, and thus he chose to let Christ live His Life out through him. Even though he had no human love left for the guard, Jesus did. And that's all that mattered. As we saw, the guard was unable to resist it.

## "Not My Will, But Thine"

As Christians then, we can be honest with God and say, "I don't understand why You have allowed this tragedy to happen in my life." "I don't feel Your presence." "I am doubtful that You are leading me to do this." "I am fearful of what is going to happen." "I don't want to love this person anymore. I don't want to forgive them. He has hurt me beyond repair. I despise him right now. *But*, I know I have Your authority to say, like Jesus did in Matthew 26:39, 'Not my will [not my natural feelings and desires], but Thine.'"

As we said before, we have been so programmed to "feel" everything we choose, that when we don't "feel" our choices, we don't think they're genuine. In God's Kingdom, however, this does <u>not</u> have to be the case. Christians don't have to be carried on by the "tide of emotion" anymore, like non-believers, because we have God's authority, not only to choose what He desires, but also His power to perform His desires in our lives—regardless of how we feel.

This, to me, is one of the most incredible gifts of all. I don't have to "feel" my choices; I just have to be willing to make them. God then does the rest.

## "I Love You More Than the Carpeting"

About 15 years ago, we bought our "dream house" in Big Bear Lake, California. It needed, however, some extensive remodeling. We actually moved out of most of the house and gutted it. There was only one bedroom, one bathroom, and a back porch left to live in during the remodeling.

The remodeling job was supposed to take only about six months. The contractor had promised that it would be finished by October 31. But, like many remodeling jobs, it wasn't actually finished until the middle of December. I was planning on having ten people stay with us for Christmas, beginning December 22. It was going to be a pretty big job to move all the furniture back into the house, put up the Christmas tree and all the decorations, and prepare the rooms for the guests in such a short period of time.

Finally, on December 19, the house was finished. The workers said they would help me move the furniture back into the rooms because Chuck was away working. I had become very close friends with the builder, the head contractor, and all the helpers. After all, we had "lived together" for eight months. I especially liked Red, the head contractor. We had had long conversations about God. None of the workers knew God personally, so I had many opportunities to witness, not only with words, but with my life.

That last day, however, everyone's tempers were very short. The men were all eager to wrap everything up and get to their homes for Christmas. In our haste, many things began to go wrong:

First, I had stored all my furniture in a room off the garage and had placed all my precious valuables (crystal, china, pictures, etc.) on top of the furniture, because I knew "I" would be the one moving it all back into the house. When all four guys began to move the furniture, they moved everything so quickly I couldn't get the precious valuables off the furniture fast enough. I asked them to stop and give me five minutes so I could move all the breakables into the closest bedroom. I quickly laid all my pictures, crystal, china, and other valuables all over the bedroom floor because there wasn't time nor any furniture to put them neatly on shelves.

Then I went back and continued to move the furniture with the men. When we finished moving everything, I went back into the bedroom where I had left all my breakables on the floor. As I opened the door, I found two painters inside with an extra long aluminum ladder. They had gone in and out of that bedroom several times in order to paint the patio outside. In order to get to the patio, they had stepped in and around all my precious things on the floor. When they told me what they had done, I nearly died. Talk about "bulls in a china shop!" Combat boots, aluminum ladders and crystal don't go together!

Next, the wallpaper man came to hang the last two strips of wallpaper in my kitchen. Going back to where he had stored the leftover wallpaper the night before, he found that the "gutter" people (drain pipe people) had come in, thought it was trash and had walked all over the stored wallpaper. Needless to say, I was furious. This now meant I had to reorder two more rolls of wallpaper; and, of course, my kitchen would not be finished for Christmas!

Lastly, Red, my favorite contractor, decided to spray paint the living room fireplace black without putting any protective plastic around it or down on the floor. Now, just the night before, we had laid brand-new white berber carpeting in the living room, and I had spent two hours that morning dusting and waxing my white upholstered furniture that had been stored for eight months. As I came into the living room, having just heard about my wallpaper being ruined, I saw a cloud of "black mist" settling down all over my white upholstery and carpet. I ran to the coffee table, put my hand over its surface, and held it up. It was solid black!

How would you have responded at this point? Would you have screamed and yelled, told him he was an idiot and to get out of your house? Man, I sure felt like it! By worldly standards I certainly would have been justified. What he had done was stupid and careless! But, if I had done that, the witness I had so carefully tried to "live" the past eight months would have been destroyed. In that split second (in my mind) I turned to God and expressed how angry and upset I was. But I also told Him that I didn't want to act out of my anger and ruin what He had particularly done in Red's heart. So I gave Him my wild feelings and negative thoughts, and asked Him how I should respond.

I looked at Red and the Holy Spirit prompted me to say, "Red, I am really upset and angry now because there is black paint all over my living room carpet and furniture. I know this job could have been done three days ago when there was no furniture or carpeting in here. But I want you to know something, I love you more than the furniture and the carpeting!" And, with that, I just turned around and quietly began to clean up the mess.

When we really give our feelings and our circumstances to God, He comes up with the most creative and ingenious solutions! *I never would have thought of that response myself!* And I'm so glad God helped me hold my tongue because, by this time, all the other guys had gathered around watching the whole scene. They then began shaking their heads at Red, calling him names. I didn't need to say a thing because they called him much better names than I could have ever thought of!

Again, we don't have to "feel" our choices, we just have to be willing to make them and God does the rest! It's only our faith choices or our "contrary choices" that will allow us to experience God's Life, in spite of everything that is going on.

Everyone, of course, always wants to know what happened to my white carpeting and upholstery in that house? Well, they were both a little gray for the remainder of our stay there. But, this is the house that we eventually lost through bankruptcy, so it's now the new owners' problem.

## Faith Is Not A Feeling

Faith is not a feeling: it's simply the power to believe. Faith is the ability to see everything that happens to us through God's eyes. The only way our eyes ever get dim is by sin and self. This is why Scripture always exhorts us to walk by faith, not by sight.

Only through faith will everything eventually be turned to sight and understanding, and only through faith will we be freed from all things "seen." Only through faith can a human being leave his familiar comfort zone and move out into the realm of the unknown. Hebrews 11 is a powerful chronicle of those who faithfully stepped out into the unknown by listening to, choosing and obeying the voice of the Lord: *By faith* Noah prepared an ark...*by faith* Abraham went out...*by faith* Sarah received the ability to conceive...*by faith* Moses kept the passover...*by faith* the people of God passed through the Red Sea...*by faith* the walls of Jericho fell down...*by faith* Rahab the harlot did not perish.

Only faith can give us the strength to lay aside our own agenda and choose to stand on the solid foundation that is Christ. Noah laid aside his reputation to build the ark; Abraham laid aside his wealth and property to follow God into the desert; Moses laid aside the treasures of Egypt to pursue his destiny; and Rahab laid aside her cultural identity to seek refuge with the people of God. In every case, these men and women chose to follow God in a completely "unreasonable" route, allowing their faith to silence all protest coming from their own thoughts and emotions.

Hebrews 11 tells us that all these men and women were "warriors" of the faith, simply because they chose His will over their own.

Faith, as we said before, simply comes in the form of a "choice."

(If you want to explore the subject of faith, especially having faith in difficult times, I would suggest getting the book *Faith in the Night Seasons* and researching Chapter Five.)

## Make Faith Choices a Habit

Moment by moment, then, we have the awesome responsibility of either choosing to "walk after the Spirit" and doing what God has asked or choosing to "walk by the flesh" and following our own desires. (Romans 7:25; 8:5) We can define the "flesh" as everything that occurs in our soul and body that is "not of the Spirit" or "not of faith." Walking after the flesh means that we have made emotional choices to follow what *we* desire over what God has called us to do, and thus, our self-life (rather than God's Life) has taken over. At this point, it's our own image that is being portrayed to the world and not Christ's. This is what causes those watching to be confused, because we proclaim to be Christians, and yet we're not acting Christ-like. Yes, we are still Christians, but it's certainly not Christ's Life that is showing forth.

Just like it's been a habit all our lives to make emotional choices, we must now begin to make a habit of making faith choices. Most of our lives we haven't even thought about the choices we've made; we've just reacted and done whatever we've felt like. Now, we must reverse that chain reaction, begin to take every thought captive (2 Corinthians 10:5) and recognize the choices that are before us, understanding that it's going to take some time to re-establish new habit patterns.

Old habit patterns (i.e., conditioned responses) are hard to break because they are in our "comfort zone." Making choices that we don't feel and that we don't want to make, is going to be foreign and unfamiliar for awhile and stretch us to the max. We mustn't expect an easy or a quick transition, but, we must persevere anyway and not let the enemy dissuade us. God is faithful and He promises, if we do our part, He will set us free.

Many years ago, a woman at one of my retreats had some great advice for all of us. She had a severely retarded child. She said that when she first found out about her son being handicapped, she began to worry about what would happen when he began to walk. Could she handle him? What would happen when he began school? And what about when he became a teenager? Adulthood, etc.?

She told us a dear friend gave her the best advice ever: *"Take one day at a time. Don't think and worry about how to handle the future. Just make the appropriate choices for today and allow God to give you the strength and power you need."*

That's good advice for us also. Jesus even tells us there's enough evil in one day to be concerned about, without looking ahead. (Matthew 6:34) In other words, take one day at a time and make the appropriate choices that that day brings. Choose to "cast down imaginations, and every high thing that exalteth itself against the knowledge of God, and bring into captivity every thought to the obedience of Christ; *and have a readiness to revenge* [deal with] *all disobedience...*" (2 Corinthians 10:5-6) God knows the perfect way and the perfect timing to reveal truth to us. We just need to be willing to hear it, and then deal with it. He will do the rest.

Remember, even our friends and our counselors can't make these kinds of choices for us. They can only hold us, pray for us and lead us to Christ, but, in the end, we are the ones who must make the appropriate choices. God wants all of us cleansed and healed, conformed into His image, "filled with intimate knowledge of Him" and walking in His Love. Over time, making these kinds of non-feeling choices will become a habit.

## An Example: "I Had That Message Once"

Even though I have walked this way for over 20 years, I could easily stop choosing God's way today and in a very short time, I would be right back where I started. Listen to this example:

I had lunch with a dear friend several years ago who had done this very thing—stopped choosing. After many years of walking in the Spirit, a situation had occurred in her life that was completely overwhelming, and so she simply stopped making faith choices. She became almost numb from the rejection and betrayal she was feeling, and slowly the enemy was allowed to rebuild old strongholds that had once been destroyed. As she began to experience old problems she thought she had already dealt with years ago, it almost drove her to despair. As a result, she began to doubt God's faithfulness.

What she didn't realize was that because *she* had stopped taking every thought captive, and *she* had stopped making contrary choices, *she* was the one who allowed new, ungodly things to be reprogrammed back into her once-cleansed soul. Thus, it wasn't God who was unfaithful, *she* was the one who had quenched His Spirit and allowed the enemy an entrance to her soul.

Consequently, we must learn to think first, not just "react." We need to think and then respond the way God would have us to by making faith choices to do His will, regardless of whatever is going on in our lives. After repeated use, this new way of thinking, choosing and responding will become first nature.

## M & M's

Ephesians 5:17-18 says, "Be ye not unwise, but understand what the will of the Lord is. ...[That ye] be [*being*] filled with the Spirit [all day, every day]."

In other words, it's our *constant* choice to be filled with His Spirit. It's not just a one-time event! Sanctification is a process, and it's a process that we will be in for the rest of our lives. Unfortunately, there's just no room for coasting—it's a moment-by-moment faith walk. In fact, there is no such thing as *standing still* in our walk with God. We are either moving ahead or falling behind.

I once had an old friend come up to me and say, "Nan, I had hold of this message once." I obviously asked him, "What happened?" He said, "It's too hard and I just let go." I really understood his answer because moment-by-moment faith choices <u>are</u> hard to make and you can *never* stop making them, as seen in the above example! You can never rest. You can never coast! And, for many, this is just too high a price to pay. But, let me ask you a very important question: What's the alternative? It's literally "life" or "death." See Deuteronomy 30:19-20. This young man had made his choice. He's now back on heavy drugs, has lost his wife and children and is completely destitute.

A few years ago, I spoke in Northern California and the precious sisters there decided to call these kinds of moment-by-moment choices, their "M & M's." They not only gave me a box of real M & M's, they also made me a beautiful embroidered picture with the letters M & M in the center to remind me of these kinds of constant choices.

James 1:3-4 declares, "Knowing this, that the trying of your faith [these constant M & M choices] worketh patience. But let patience have her perfect work, that ye may be perfect and entire, wanting nothing."

In other words, the end result is worth all of the trouble!

## God Changes Our Feelings

Something important to point out here, is that we are <u>not</u> responsible to change our negative feelings.  There's no way we can do that!  We're only responsible to put in charge the Person who <u>can</u> change our feelings, and that, of course, is God.  And we do this by, again, making faith choices.  God, then, in His perfect timing and way, changes our feelings and our thoughts to match the faith choices we have made and makes us genuine. In other words, *He aligns our feelings with our choices.*

Again, we are so programmed to *feel* everything we choose, and when we don't feel our choices we often don't think they are genuine.  It makes us feel like phonies.  However, in God's kingdom, this is not the case.  Christians have the supernatural ability within them (because of the indwelling Spirit of God) to go against what they think, feel and desire because God has given us the *authority* in Scripture to do so.  He also has given us the supernatural *power* to perform those non-feeling choices in our lives (i.e., to implement something different than how we feel).

Mark 9:24 validates this:  "Lord, I believe; [now] help Thou mine unbelief."  In other words, "Lord, I choose to believe by faith what You promise [contrary choice]; now I trust You to make my feelings align with that choice and perform it in my life."

## An Example:  Rats, Spiders and Insects

I have a dear friend, Leona, who used to be a missionary in Bangkok, Thailand. Out of pure desperation, Leona learned how to make contrary choices. The first year she was in Thailand was absolutely miserable for her. She was allergic to much of the Thai food and would get violently ill every time she ate some. She also hated the hot, sticky, and muggy weather, the huge spiders and insects, and the abundance of rats and crawling vermin that infested most of the buildings.

In addition to these problems, Leona didn't know the Thai language, so she was extremely lonely. She had no permanent church home, so there was no one for her to turn to for spiritual help, for encouragement or just plain friendship except, of course, the Lord.

Over and over again by faith, with absolutely no feelings at all, she made choices to trust that God <u>had</u> sent her there for a reason and a purpose. Continually, she chose to give God her emotional feelings about her environment (rather than be consumed by them), and to follow Him. Eventually, the Lord aligned her feelings with what she had so faithfully chosen, and He was able to accomplish all that He had planned through her.

What was so exciting for me, was to witness her change of heart. From the first year where she hated everything that had to do with Thailand, to where in the end, I heard her say over and over again, "I can't wait to get home to Thailand. I miss my friends, the food and, yes, even the bugs and the weather."

Contrary choices really do work! Someone recently called it "the habit of choice." And I think that's very appropriate! Our only responsibility is to make the appropriate choices; God then is the one who will change our thoughts and emotions and make us genuine.

## All We Need to Be Is "Willing"

A friend called a few weeks ago and said, "Nancy, I am hurting so badly I don't even *want to* make the right choices." She has been drowning in physical pain for almost a year, with very little relief.

I felt so badly for her, but I knew I needed to exhort her. "Dear friend, you don't have to *want to* make the right choice, you simply must be *willing to* make them. 'Not wanting to' is the same thing as saying 'I don't feel like' making the right choice. God never said that we had to *want to* or *feel like* making that choice; He just said we *must be willing* to make that choice."

Isaiah 1:19 promises, "If ye be willing and obedient, ye shall eat of the good of the land." It doesn't say, "if you feel willing," it just says "be willing!" Even if we are saying under our breath, "I don't want to, I don't feel like it and I don't understand it, but nevertheless, I am willing!"

People often ask me, "If I really didn't mean the choice I made, is it still genuine to God? Is it real to Him?" What they are asking is, because they didn't feel their choice, does it count with God? Absolutely! You're just saying like Jesus did, "Not my will, but Thine." You're simply being honest with Him and, besides, He knows it anyway. In His economy, it's always "by faith and not feelings."

## A Holding Pattern

Now sometimes God changes our feelings to align with our faith choices immediately, and when this happens it's powerful; but other times it takes a period of days, or even weeks, where we must walk by faith, without feeling anything. The amount of time that the healing process takes, seems to depend upon how deep our wound is and how long it has been in us. In other words, the deeper the hurt, the longer the process (for our feelings to align with our choices) seems to take. I call this in-between time— that period of time *before* my feelings are aligned, but after I have made the right choices—my "holding pattern." It's also analogous to being shot with an arrow. You can remove the arrow immediately, but it still takes time before you will "feel" the healing. And it's the same with our spiritual lives.

Most of the things that we give over to the Lord are of the flesh and will go away pretty quickly if we are faithful to do our part. But some of the things that will come up are long-standing strongholds of the enemy, and he won't let these go quickly. So don't be dismayed if feelings from these things do reappear.

Actually, God takes our negative thoughts and feelings the moment we choose to give them to Him, but often our feelings don't align with that choice for awhile. And this is where Satan tries to make us think that God isn't faithful and that He hasn't taken them. Satan wants to use this in-between time to destroy us. God often lets us go for awhile to test our faith and to strengthen us. Will we keep on believing Him even though, for awhile, we don't see any evidence of change?

*Again, the deeper the wound, the longer it will take for our feelings to align with our choices.*

## Knowing God Loves Us

In our haste to be "like Jesus," so often we forget the very first basic step, which is to know the extent and the depth of God's Love for us personally. If we really knew how much God loves us, there would never be any reason to fear what He might allow into our lives. We would just have the confidence and the trust to continually abandon our lives into His cares, and know he will take care of us no matter what.

God's Love is a gift that we all receive when we are born anew by His Spirit. Therefore, if you have asked Jesus into your heart as your Savior, then not only Jesus is in your heart, but His Love is there also. John 17:26 validates this: "And I have declared... that the Love wherewith Thou [Father] hast loved Me [Jesus] may be in them, and I in them."

Therefore, *before* we can go any further in our walk with the Lord, we need to know without a shadow of a doubt, that we are loved and that He has given us the authority and the power to make choices we don't feel: then we'll have the confidence and the trust to lay our wills and our lives down before Him.

"When thou passest through the waters [trouble], I will be with thee; and through the rivers, they shall not overflow thee; when thou walkest through the fire, thou shalt not be burned; neither shall the flame kindle upon thee. For I am the Lord thy God...[You are] precious in My sight and...I have loved thee." (Isaiah 43:2-4)

When I first began teaching about "faith choices" in *The Way of Agape,* my focus was on the two great commandments: "Thou shalt love the Lord thy God with all thy heart, and with all thy soul, and with all thy mind...and thou shalt love thy neighbour as thyself." (Matthew 22:37-39)

After several years of hearing the reactions of the women in those first classes, however, I realized that there is no way that they could learn to surrender themselves completely to God and love others, until they *first* personally knew that God loved them. Knowing that God loves us is the *foundation* of our faith walk. In other words, without first being able to experience His Love and acceptance for ourselves, we're <u>never</u> going to be able to move forward in our Christian life.

## God's Love Is Our Foundation

Simply put, it's impossible to lay our lives down to someone if we don't really think that they love us. This principle is true no matter how long we have been Christians, no matter how many people we have led to the Lord, no matter how many Scriptures we know or how many Bible studies we have taught. If we know that God loves us, then we'll have the confidence and the trust to continually relinquish our wills and our lives to Him, and have that daily experience of seeing His Love for us at every turn. As Isaiah 49:16 says, "Behold, I have graven thee upon the palms of My hands; thy walls [our souls] are continually before Me."

If we doubt His Love, however, then we won't have the confidence to surrender ourselves, which will limit not only our ability to experience His personal touch on our own lives, but also His Love to others.

Now, this doesn't mean that God isn't in our hearts, loving us. He is! It just means that because we have quenched His Spirit by doubting that Love, we won't have that daily, living experience of encountering His handprint at every turn.

This holds true for making faith choices as well.

If we know God loves us, we'll have the confidence to make choices we don't feel, because we know He'll be faithful to take our real feelings away, fill us with His Love and perform His will through us. If we're not sure He loves us, our real feelings will scream, "It's scary. Don't do it. I'm afraid. How do I know God will be faithful? I'm not sure! I can't."

(If you have trouble believing that God loves you and will be faithful to perform what He has promised to you, I strongly suggest getting *The Way of Agape* textbook and specifically reading Chapter Seven, "How Do I Know God Loves Me?" You might also go over the *Knowing God Loves* Me Scriptures in the Appendix and, by faith, choose to believe what God says in those Scriptures.)

## How Far Are You Willing to Go?

I just got off the phone talking with a young man facing total financial ruin. He has tried everything he can think of to turn the situation around, but nothing has helped. He is now at the very bottom. He told me, "God must not love me, because I have sought Him every day, but I don't hear a thing back. I'm at the end of my road because I don't know where to turn now."

Trials often do come upon us suddenly and often without advance warning. If we know that God loves us, know how to make choices to continually relinquish ourselves to Him and trust Him, then we'll be able to experience His presence, even in the midst of the trial. If, however, we don't know His Love personally, don't have the confidence to surrender ourselves to Him in faith and don't trust Him, then, rather than experiencing His presence, doubt and unbelief will prevail and eventually, cause us to fall away from faith. Doubt in God's faithfulness and His Love will affect every choice we make, and nothing will bring us down faster.

It's imperative to understand that God loves us so much that He gave us His Life (1 John 3:16). He loves us so much He yearns to show us what His will is. *And, only He knows what that will is and what it will take to implement it in our lives.* In other words, everything He allows in our lives, good or bad (from our point of view), is to accomplish that will. All of the circumstances of our lives come only by permission of our loving Father. If we truly believe this, then we can make the appropriate choices. If we don't, then we have no basis upon which to place our faith or trust.

In our dark seasons of life (like what the young man above is going through), God doesn't ask us to understand everything that He is doing, *but simply to trust and believe in His Love through what He is doing.* Because this young man has begun to doubt God's Love, he has lost the confidence and the trust he needs to continually surrender his life to the Lord and thus, he has curtailed personally experiencing God's Love.

You see the vicious circle that occurs in so many of our lives: because we doubt His Love, we can't trust Him enough to relinquish our wills and our lives, thus, we stop making faith choices and, instead, begin to follow our own thoughts and emotions. At that point, we take our eyes off of the Lord and begin to look at the situation we find ourselves in, and, as a result, we become overwhelmed and the enemy rejoices.

## God's Severe Mercy

When I first read the term "severe mercy" in C.S. Lewis's writings, it really confused me. But, since experiencing God's severe mercy in my own life, I see its importance. God's Love, in the Old Testament, is called *chesed* in the Hebrew and it means, not only His *loving and compassionate Love* (His mercy), but also His *strict* (severe) *and discipline Love*. In other words, His severe mercy. Both of these aspects typify God's Love. Just as we, as parents, must love our children with tough love, God often must do the same with us. Now, that doesn't mean that He loves us any less. *In fact, most of the time, it means He loves us more*!

One of the great 16th century saints said, "The more God loves us, the less He spares us."[1]

Most of us know *in our heads* that God loves us, but very few of us really know how much He loves us in our everyday lives. And because of this, when trials and troubles occur and we don't see or feel His Love, we become unable to lay our wills down and make choices by faith.

Therefore, it's critical to the point where we know that no matter what it looks like to us, the Lord will never allow anything to happen to us or in our lives that is not "Father filtered," and we can trust Him to work out His purposes in our lives in His perfect way.

## Do You Really "Know" God?

Let me ask you a personal question. Do you really know God? Now, I don't mean "intellectual knowledge" or "head knowledge," I mean that moment-by-moment intimacy that only a loving Father and child can experience. Sadly, most Christians know *about* Him, but they're not intimately acquainted with His character or with His daily "loving" touch upon their lives.

*To know God means to have living experience* of Him. The Greek word for this kind of knowledge is ***oida,*** which comes from the root word ***eidon,*** meaning "to see" and "to experience." To know God means to see and experience His Life through us.

1 John 5:13 promises, "These things have I written unto you that believe on the name of the Son of God; that ye may know [have living experience] that ye have eternal life." And 1 Corinthians 2:12 declares, "Now we have received, not the spirit of the world, but the spirit which is of God; that we might know [have living experience of] the things that are freely given to us of God."

## Our Only Hope for the Future

When we begin to know God in this way, then we'll never fear the circumstances that He allows into our lives. We'll know that everything in our lives is "Father filtered" and will be used for His purposes. Remember Job 13:15, which tells us, "Though He slay me, yet will I trust in Him." With all the horrendous things that God had allowed in his life, how could Job say that? He could say it because he knew, without a shadow of a doubt, that God loved Him.

Making faith choices not only allows us to experience more of God's Love for others, but it allows us to personally experience His Love to a much greater degree. And this is what will give us that consistent hope for the future—hope which leads us to faith and belief and the ability to trust Him in all things.

Hope in God's Love is what will help us endure, persevere and hang on through the trials, the pain and the suffering; hope in God's Love is what will give us the faith to *go against the tide of emotion;* and, hope in His Love is what will help us look beyond the near term, beyond the current situation, beyond the horrendous problems, and look to Christ for our final victory. If we know without a doubt that we are loved by the Father, then there is always hope for the future!

"Behold, I have graven thee upon the palms of My hands; thy walls [thy soul] are continually before Me." (Isaiah 49:16)

## Endnote:

1. *The Seeking Heart*, Francois Fenelon, page 73.

# Chapter Six
## *Emotional Choices*

Here's a story from one of David Wilkerson's newsletters,[1] that, to me, perfectly illustrates the danger of emotional choices:

"In 1921, two young missionary couples in Stockholm, Sweden, received a burden to go to the Belgian Congo (which is now Zaire). David and Svea Flood (along with their 2-year old son) joined Joel and Bertha Erickson to battle insects, fierce heat, malaria and malnutrition. But after six months in the jungle, they had made little or no contact with the native people. Although the Erickson's decided to return to the mission station, the Flood's chose to stay in their lonely outpost. Svea was now pregnant and sick with malaria, yet she faithfully continued to minister to their one and only convert, a little boy from one of the nearby villages.

"Svea died after giving birth to a healthy baby girl, and as David Flood stood over his beloved wife's grave, he poured out his bitterness to God: 'Why did You allow this? We came here to give our lives, and now my wife is dead at 27! All we have to show for all this is one little village boy who probably doesn't even understand what we've told him. You've failed me, God. What a waste of life!'

"David Flood ended up making drastic "emotional choices:" he chose to leave his new daughter with the Erickson's; took his son back home with him to Sweden; and, from then on, never allowed the name of "God" to be mentioned in his presence. His little girl was raised in the Congo by an American missionary couple, who named their adopted daughter "Aggie."

"Throughout her life, Aggie tried to locate her real father, but her letters were never answered. She never knew that David Flood had remarried and fathered four more children, and she never knew that he had plunged into despair and had become a total alcoholic. But when she was in her forties, Aggie and her husband were given round-trip tickets to Sweden, and while spending a day's layover in London, the couple went to hear a well-known black preacher from the Belgian Congo.

"After the meeting, Aggie asked the preacher, 'Did you ever know David and Svea Flood?' To her great surprise, he answered, 'Svea Flood led me to the Lord when I was a little boy.' Aggie was ecstatic to learn that her mother's only convert was being mightily used to evangelize Zaire, and he was overjoyed to meet the daughter of the woman who had introduced him to Christ.

"When Aggie arrived in Sweden, she located her father in an impoverished area of Stockholm, living in a rundown apartment filled with empty liquor bottles. David Flood was now a 73-year old diabetic who had had a stroke and whose eyes were covered with cataracts, yet when she identified herself, he began to weep and apologize for abandoning her. But when Aggie said, 'That's okay, Daddy. God took care of me,' he became totally enraged.

"'God didn't take care of you!' he cried. 'He ruined our whole family! He led us to Africa and then betrayed us! Nothing ever came of our time there, and it was a waste of our lives!'

"That's when Aggie told him about the black preacher she'd just met in London, and how the Congo had been evangelized through the efforts of his wife's one and only convert. As he listened to his daughter, the Holy Spirit suddenly fell on David Flood, and tears of sorrow and repentance began to flow down his face. Although God mercifully restored him before he died, David Flood left behind five unsaved and embittered children. *His anger towards God had totally wasted his life's potential, and created a tragic legacy for his family.*"

-------------------

This story clearly illustrates the danger of going with *the tide of emotion* and following our own thoughts and desires. Had David Flood chosen by an act of his will to accept the situation as coming directly from the hand of God, who knows what awesome fruit God could have brought forth from his life? *God is involved in every aspect of our existence, and there is no sorrow so great that He cannot somehow "recycle" it to bring forth a blessing.* The deciding factor, however, is our choice to release God to work in our lives.

## Nothing Shall Separate Us

The above story exemplifies quite graphically, that when we make emotional choices to follow our own desires over God's will, we quench His Spirit, and thus, won't *experience* His Love either for ourselves or for others.

Psalm 119:70 explains this further. It tells us that when we make emotional choices, our hearts become "fat as grease" (like kitchen lard!). This grease then, not only clogs, chokes out and quenches any communication or personal leading from God, it also causes us to become insensitive and unfeeling towards others. This is where James tells us that the "pure water" of God's Spirit gets blocked off and comes out bitter. (James 3:10-11)

It's interesting to note that when you put grease or fat on a physical burn, you not only make that area insensitive and resistant to healing, you also cause a scar to be formed in its place. Sin and self are just like that grease—they not only make us insensitive and resistant to God's leading, but they also leave scars on our lives. In other words, we always reap the consequences of our wrong choices, as clearly seen in the above story about Aggie.

## What Is Sin?

The Bible tells us that "sin" is anything that causes us to be separated from God or anything that is not of faith. As Isaiah 59:2 states, "Your iniquities have separated between you and your God, and your sins have hid His face from you, that He will not hear." (Romans 14:23c)

When I used to think of sin, I thought of the list in Galatians 5:19-21 and I could say, "Hey, I'm really okay. I don't do those kinds of things!" But, then I came across a little book called *The Calvary Road* by Roy Hession that changed my life. In this little book, there is a list of subtle things that cover our hearts and separate us from God's Life, just as much as the big ones of Galatians 5. Let me recall just a few:

"*Self-pity, self-defensiveness, oversensitivity, criticalness, resentfulness, worry, grumbling, bossiness, self-complacency, self-energy, self-seeking, self-indulgence, self-consciousness.*"

If any of you reading this, do <u>not</u> experience any of these things, then you may close this book now. You have no need of this teaching.

The above list describes sins that quench God's Spirit and cover our hearts just as much as the "biggies" of Galatians 5. These "little sins" cover our hearts with grease, form a barrier or a blockage and prohibit God's Life from being experienced not only in our lives (our souls), but also *through us* to others.

## An Example: "Could I Borrow Some Money?"

Joanne, an extreme perfectionist, used to be a hairdresser in a Christian salon. She never could stand any untidiness or messiness in her booth.

Joanne had a friend named Susie, who worked in the booth next to hers. Susie was a single mom, who out of necessity (when her babysitter did not show up) brought her two little children to work with her. Of course, the kids often brought crackers and cookies, and before long the whole place would become a total disaster.

Joanne tried to put up with this situation for a while. She smiled and pretended everything was fine, even sometimes taking care of Susie's children. But after months of this inconvenience, the constant mess really got to her, and she unknowingly allowed deep roots of bitterness to grow.

Like many of us, Joanne didn't realize that when we don't deal with our real negative thoughts and emotions right away, they form a barrier (grease) over our hearts and can become the motivation for many of our actions.

One day while out shopping, Joanne ran into Susie who was trying to buy some lingerie. Susie's estranged husband was coming over the next night for a visit, and Susie was hoping there might be a chance for a reconciliation. When Susie went to pay for the lingerie, however, the cashier wouldn't take her credit card and she had no cash, so she quickly turned to Joanne and asked, "Please, could I borrow some money? I'll pay you back at work in the morning."

Before Joanne could even think, she responded with, "No, I'm really sorry, but..." and then she made up some feeble excuse for why she couldn't loan Susie the money. Joanne actually had plenty of money in her purse, but because her heart was so clogged by undealt-with resentment and bitterness, she reacted out of that *grease*, rather than God's Love.

Susie responded, "Oh, I understand. I was just hoping to make tomorrow night special. It's okay." And then she left. Joanne was mortified. She could hardly believe what just came out of her mouth. She could have easily lent Susie the money, because she had plenty in her purse.

Guilt and shame consumed her. She finally went to the ladies' room to regain her composure. In the bathroom, she wept, asking the Lord to forgive her. He exposed the bitterness and resentment that she was still harboring in her heart against Susie for always bringing her children to work. Joanne thanked God for revealing the truth, chose to confess and repent of it and then, to give it over to the Lord, knowing that He would forgive her and cleanse her.

When she left the bathroom and went back into the store, she saw Susie's pile of lingerie still sitting there on the counter. Prompted by the Holy Spirit, she bought the lingerie as a gift for Susie. When Joanne went to work the next morning, she told Susie the whole story, asked her forgiveness and then gave her the "love gift" out of her heart. Once again "the sweet fountain water" of God's Life in Joanne's heart was able to flow. (James 3:10-11)

When we daily wash our hearts with that cool, fresh, running water of God's Word by confessing, repenting, and giving our sins to God, our sin and our self will not only be washed away, but no scars will be left!

## Chain Reaction of Our Soul

One of the more interesting things I learned when I was writing *Be Ye Transformed*, is that there is a natural "chain reaction" in each of our souls. We have briefly mentioned this before, but if we could peel back the outer layer of our soul, we would see that our *thoughts* trigger our *emotions*; our emotions then stir up our *desires*; and our desires produce our *actions*. In other words, every action we take really comes from four split decisions.

Since our thoughts are the first to be triggered in this chain-reaction, God, throughout Scripture, puts great emphasis on them. He knows that if we can catch the negative thoughts when they first occur, then we'll be able to stop the whole chain reaction before it even begins. And, we might even be able to prevent some of the sin before it occurs in our lives.

What happens, however, when we *don't* take every thought captive, is that we end up being carried on by the tide of emotion (that chain reaction), quenching God's Spirit, and then, His Life in our hearts is thwarted. This is why 2 Corinthians 10:5 exhorts us to: "...bring into captivity every thought to the obedience of Christ." In other words, we are to stop and examine the thoughts we have.

Now, obviously, we can't examine every thought that we think, but we *can* stop and take a good hard look at the angry thoughts, the hurtful thoughts, the fearful thoughts, etc. Any thought that takes away our peace is a thought God wants us to "take captive" and examine.

If we're unable to catch the negative thoughts before they stir up our emotions, then, perhaps we can spot the wild emotions before they become out-of-control desires, or the self-centered desires before they become actions. Again, it's like splitting hairs to examine this chain reaction, but it's imperative that we see its domino *effect*. It's called the *tide of our emotions*.

## An Example: David

A Scriptural example of this chain reaction is again King David in 2 Samuel 11. David, as we mentioned in Chapter Four, was on his roof top when he saw Bathsheba bathing next door. He *thought* to himself how absolutely beautiful she was. But, rather than catch those natural thoughts when they first occurred, he allowed them to stir up his lustful *emotions,* which in turn, fed his desires and finally, influenced his *actions*.

He sent his servants to inquire after the woman. They reported back to him that she was Bathsheba, wife of Uriah. But, that didn't stop David. He was already immersed in his lustful thinking and thus, he chooses to act upon these desires and sent for Bathsheba. And, you know the rest of the story.

David, to me, is not only a perfect example of a double-minded Christian, but also an example of a believer who, because he was totally immersed in the tide of his own emotional thinking, didn't take his thoughts captive and thus, God's Life in him was completely quenched. And, the same thing can be true of us. If we let the negative thought in, sinful or self-centered actions will result. This is why the battle is for our minds. As we said before, whoever controls our thinking, will ultimately control our lives.

Jesus, as God in fully human form, was able to live the perfect sinless life, because He was able to perfectly control His thoughts, emotions, desires and actions. In other words, He was able to catch every negative thought *before* it triggered the negative chain reaction. Thus, His Thoughts were perfectly Spirit-controlled. While I don't believe we will ever be able to do this perfectly (only Jesus could), He has given us an example to follow.

## When Are Thoughts "Sin?"

Technically we are not responsible for the first, original self-centered or ungodly thought when it first pops into our minds; *it's what we choose to do with that thought that produces the sin or not.* If we can recognize the negative thought and choose immediately to give it over to God, then we'll not have sinned. However, if we entertain, mull over and follow what those thoughts are prompting us to do, then, obviously, it will be sin and we'll end up with that layer of grease covering our hearts.

Interestingly, even if we do nothing with our negative thinking, it will *still* end up quenching God's Spirit and eventually be buried in the hidden part of our soul. Remember, it's impossible to stand still in our walk with God; we are either moving forward with Him or falling behind.

Consequently, the original, negative thought itself is not sin. It's simply a normal and natural part of our being human. The sin occurs when we choose to follow what those thoughts are telling us to do over what God has prompted. And, even if we simply entertain those thoughts in our minds, rather than giving them to God, we still will quench His Spirit in us.

God declares in Ephesians 4:29-32 that it is absolutely imperative that we not even contemplate bad thoughts about others, let alone speak them. "Let no corrupt communication proceed out of your mouth, but that which is good to the use of edifying, that it may minister grace unto the hearers. And grieve not the Holy Spirit of God, whereby ye are sealed unto the day of redemption. *Let all bitterness, and wrath, and anger, and clamour, and evil speaking, be put away from you, with all malice: And be ye kind one to another, tender-hearted, forgiving one another, even as God for Christ's sake hath forgiven you."*

## Grieve Not the Holy Spirit

Another translation of the above Ephesians 4 Scripture says: "Let nothing come forth out of our mouth that does not edify the hearers." One of the things that God has impressed on my heart lately, is the importance of not sharing anything that does not edify the hearer, *even if that hearer is my own family*. In other words, when we complain out loud about another person or situation, especially to our family, if it doesn't "lift the hearer up" or "bring him closer to God," then it's sin. Sharing our innermost thoughts, especially with our husbands or our grown children, is so natural. It's like talking to ourselves. However, if these comments are negative about others, or unedifying, then, they will grieve God's Spirit.

What happens when we share ungodly thoughts with others, is that we not only contaminate them, but we also reprogram those bad thoughts right back in the hidden part of our own soul, once again, stirring up our soulish emotions and desires. Haven't you ever experienced this? After having been with someone who complained about another person the whole time you were with them, you come away feeling polluted and tainted yourself. Thus, it's imperative that we try to catch the bad thoughts when they first come in, and deal with them ourselves, so that we don't pass them on to others. We must recognize them and then, refuse to even think them.

This is exactly what 2 Corinthians 10:5-6 means when it says, "...bringing into captivity every thought to the obedience of Christ; *And having in a readiness to revenge all disobedience, when your obedience is fulfilled."* This is simply saying, catch the negative thoughts as they come in and deal with them.

## A Classic Example:  Sara

Let me give you an incredible example of a Christian sister who, in the worst possible situations, recognized her bitterness, unforgiveness and anger, and by faith constantly chose to give these to God.

I started corresponding with Sara many years ago when she wrote and told me her incredible story.  Her two small children, a four month old baby son and a 4-year old daughter, were kidnapped by her former husband and missing for three and a half years!  God, however, performed a miracle by, first of all, saving her from personally being traumatized and buried in her emotions for those three and a half years, and next, by eventually bringing her children home.

When all of this occurred, Sara was in the process of divorcing this man, because of extreme physical abuse not only to her, but also to her children.  He had even threatened their lives.  After their separation, however, he went absolutely crazy and would not leave them alone.  He followed Sara and the children everywhere, and one day, he kidnapped the children from their day-care center.   The police became involved, but legally their hands were tied because there were no final custody papers.

One of the first things Sara said she had to deal with was *doubt*.  She was certain that God had told her to leave this emotionally unstable man and get the children away.  "Why now, had this man won?"  As Sara would choose by faith, however, to "take those negative thoughts captive" and release her doubt to the Lord, He would always minister to her that peace "that passes all understanding." Repeatedly He gave her Psalm 71, which promises that He would restore her life and put to confusion those who wanted to harm her.

Next, she said, she had to deal with *unforgiveness*. By faith—not feeling like it at all—Sara chose over and over again to unconditionally forgive her ex-husband. Soon, she said, she found herself praying for his salvation and all the hate and bitterness just seemed to fade away.

Finally, there was the *fear*. Continually, she tormented herself as she worried about her children's safety. "Do my children have a place to sleep tonight? Are they eating right? Are they well?" But again, as she would give these things over to God, His voice would always come back, "Don't you think I love your children much more than you do? Don't you think I can take care of them?"

She had to give her fears, doubts and unforgiveness over to God about 50 times a day and choose each time to trust and believe that He would be faithful to do what He had promised. As she made those faith choices, however, God always changed her negative feelings to align and gave her the strength to go on. Her continual promise from Him was, "...all things work together for good to them that love God [to those who totally give themselves over to Him]..." (Romans 8:28)

After three and a half years, a miracle happened. Through a series of events, Sara was able to locate her ex-husband and her children. At this point, the police took an active involvement in the case and the ex-husband was arrested. He was sent to prison, not only for kidnapping but also for other charges as well.

Beautiful Sara is now married to a wonderful pastor back East and has an incredible ministry of her own. Her children have had their share of problems as they have learned to deal with their past, but through the Lord, they have grown into healthy adults who love Jesus and who are learning to forgive, love and pray for their biological father.

If Sara, in the midst of this horrendous situation, can be set free of her fears, doubts and unforgiveness by making non-feeling choices, I believe any of us can! Sara is not a *super saint*, she's just like you and me. She has learned however, that choosing by faith to follow God in all circumstances is the only thing that will free us from ourselves, from others and from Satan's schemes.

Again, it's a mind battle. If Satan can just direct our thinking without our even being aware of it, by our continuing on in our own natural emotional responses, then he has got us and he doesn't need to do another thing!

## The Power of Sin

Now, one of the reasons we are so prone to making wrong, emotional choices that quench God's Life in us, is that our souls and our bodies (i.e., the *flesh*) are still dominated and controlled by what is called the "power of sin." Romans 7:21 tells us that the power of sin is the energy force that dwells in our unrenewed bodies, whose whole intent and purpose is to cause us to veer off course and to miss the mark—that of being conformed into the Image of Christ. Satan, therefore, uses the power of sin as his tool to gain access to our flesh (our souls and bodies).

No one can ever take us out of the keeping power of God's Holy Spirit once we have been born again—we *do have that eternal security*—but we can, by our own emotional choice, quench God's power in us and open our souls and bodies up to the power of sin. (Colossians 1:13-14) And, this is exactly what happens when we go with the emotional tide in our souls. Remember, David Flood in the story at the beginning of this chapter.

When we make an emotional choice, Satan (through the power of sin) not only has access to our conscious thoughts, emotions, and desires, he also has access to the things that we have pushed down and buried in the hidden recesses of our souls—all our doubts, unforgiveness, fears, roots of bitterness, insecurities and so forth. This is the enemy's "playground" and, how he tries to continually influence our choices. *It's our choices that he is after*.

## Satan's Ploy

Satan wants to get back at God, by using our emotional choices to thwart God's plans and purposes.

It's not so much that our own thoughts and emotions are warring against us, but that Satan, through the power of sin, is using them for that very purpose.

In fact, our unconfessed sins, our unresolved hurts and anger, insecurities and fears (things we haven't dealt with either because we don't want to or we don't know how) form a chain around us that binds us. These are the "handles" and the "holes" that the enemy uses to his full advantage to keep us his captives and to "revenge God."

Proverbs 5:22 is provocative in this light. "His own iniquities shall take the wicked himself, and he shall be holden [held] with the *cords of his sins*."

Because of our ignorance, not only as to how we put off our sin and self, but also the power and authority God has given us to make faith choices, Satan has been having a "field day" keeping us his prisoners.

## Emotional Choices Become Physical Ones

Here's a sad example.

Years ago, a young pastor named James, insisted upon counseling his own parishioners (including women). James had a wonderful walk with the Lord, was married to a beautiful woman and had a great family. But, he wouldn't heed the advice of his assistant pastor about the dangers that might occur through counseling the opposite sex.

Unfortunately, he underestimated Satan's ability to send an angel of light, disguised as a beautiful, but troubled young woman who "needed the personal advice of her pastor."

James was so sure of his own walk with the Lord (always a danger sign), that he unwittingly agreed to take her on. His associate pastor again strongly warned him of the obvious danger, but James was too proud to see.

Sure enough, that young woman knew exactly what to do and how to seduce James into a compromising situation. *Counseling quickly became emotional support; emotional support evolved into emotional comfort; emotional comfort developed into an emotional relationship; and that relationship quickly became physical.*

The Lord had presented James with many choices to resist, but the young self-assured pastor missed them all. When his wife found out about the affair, she blew the whistle. James not only lost his beloved wife and family, he lost his pastorate as well.

--------------------

Keep in mind that neither Satan, nor the power of sin, have access to our new spirit, our new heart or our new willpower. These areas are inviolate. He has access only to our "flesh" (our soul and body) and only, if we have given him an entrance. It's interesting to note that in the Temple of Solomon, the Holy of Holies, the Holy Place, and the Vestibule of the Porch were rooms that were also inviolate to outsiders. Only the priests could enter these rooms.

The Inner Court and the Outer Court, however, were wide open and thus, exposed to many outside influences, i.e., the dove sellers, the money changers, Satan's temptations, etc. It's fascinating to compare the architecture of the temple to our own interior makeup—heart, mind and soul. (If you would like more detailed information on this, be sure to see the books, *The Way of Agape* and *Be Ye Transformed*.)

## "Conformed To The World's Image"

God's purpose in calling us is to be conformed to His image so that others will see God's Life through us and want what we have. Satan, on the other hand, is dedicated to preventing this transformation in any way that he can, i.e. the above example. He knows that if he can just keep us *ignorant* as to the supernatural authority and power we have to *put off* self and *put on* Christ, then we'll go on depending upon our own self-centered thoughts and emotions and end up *being conformed to the world's image* and not Christ's.

A messianic *Jewish* believer wrote me a shocking letter a few years ago about how she sees Christians and how they are being conformed into the world's image, and not Christ's. I think her observations are provocative:

> "The thing that staggers me the most is that Christians don't really know that they must choose to give up every scrap of self-protective justified hurt, and that we cannot feel anything (negative) for anyone, but Christ's Love. It seems to me that most of

the Church is living "half" a Christian life. *I always wondered why Christians were not more noticeable in the world."*

I believe she is right! Most of us <u>are</u> living 'half a Christian life' because we have not been taught that all the negative things inside of us (justified or not), will not only keep us half a Christian, but will guarantee our not being noticed in this world. And you know what the reason is? *We're being conformed to the world's image and not transformed out of it into Christ's image*, as Romans 12:1-2 tells us!

"I beseech you therefore, brethren, by the mercies of God, that ye present your bodies a living sacrifice, holy, acceptable unto God, which is your reasonable service. And, be not conformed to this world: but *be ye transformed* [how?] by the renewing of your mind (by choosing to put off the old and put on the new, regardless of how we feel), that ye may prove what is that good, and acceptable, and perfect, will of God."

The only thing that will set free from the power of sin and allow us to be transformed, is learning how to make non-feeling choices to do God's will, regardless of what is going on in our lives.

## An Example: "It's Almost Impossible!"

I heard recently from a precious woman who is a pastor's wife. Linda and I have been corresponding for about 10 years.

Both Linda and her husband, Rob, grew up in the Jesus movement some 25 years ago. When they first got saved, they were "on fire" for the Lord and, when asked, eagerly became elders of a youth house. Rob eventually became the head pastor for a large church in the area. He was a great husband and father, they both were really involved in the ministry and their children saw what it meant to be "Christian." Up until 10 years ago, their marriage was a "little bit of heaven," but during the last 10 years, it has deteriorated tremendously.

Over Linda's objections, Rob decided to leave the pastorate. He became lukewarm to things of the Lord, and quickly turned to other things. At first, Linda, had tremendous hope because she remembered their first 10 years. But, when Rob continued to stay in his backslidden state, she realized that those precious years would never come back, and her hope evaporated. She became very bitter towards Rob, because she felt he was ruining their lives. Out of defense, Rob simply closed himself off from her and pursued getting a master's degree in counseling.

In Linda's most recent letter, she states, "it's so very hard not to blame him for everything because he is so blind and so self-centered. I feel like he's a hypocrite, able to counsel others, but unable to see his own problems or spend time with his own family. I constantly fight feelings of 'what might have been.'"

"Each time I seek the Lord, however, He tells me to 'forgive him and leave him to Me.' Do you know how hard that is? I can't do this myself. It's impossible! I really feel my husband has ruined my life. So, my constant choice is: forgive him and leave him to the Lord, or run with my own overwhelming and 'justified' thoughts and emotions. What do I do?"

Here's a woman faced with a hard decision and one that she must make every day, all day long: Follow her own "justified" feelings (the flesh) and quench God's Spirit, <u>or</u> follow what God has told her to do and walk in the Spirit. No one can make those difficult choices for her. But, as the Lord told me many years ago, when I ran to Him with the same question, *"Why do I have to change first?"* His answer was, *"your life depends upon it."* And, it's true, our life (before Him) depends upon our own willingness to change. We can remain where we are and stay miserable; or we can be willing to make non-feeling choices to follow what God has told us and watch Him set us free.

The goal and purpose of all our lives as Christians, as we have previously shared, is to be "conformed into His image." Thus, it doesn't matter who is the first to change, because God desires that we *all* reflect His image. Each of the circumstances He allows in our lives are simply a part of that transforming process.

Like God showed Linda, a part of our surrendering ourselves over to the Lord, moment by moment, is the choice to unconditionally forgive those who have offended us. Scripture tells us that God will be hindered from working *in* us and *in* that other person, until we release them. And, the way we release them is by unconditionally forgiving them, whether they have asked for it or not. We are not "pardoning" them; only God can do that. We are simply releasing them into His care.

As Linda expressed, it's almost impossible to forgive another person in our own strength and ability. This, however, is just another place we can trust God, regardless of how we feel (2 Corinthians 2:10). He then, not only will give us the strength we need to get through, but also the Love we need to go on as if nothing has happened.

## We Must First "See" Our Own Sin

In order to be healed, we must *first* see our own sin and self. In the above example, Rob did <u>not</u> see his own sin. David Flood in the story at the beginning of this chapter, did <u>not</u> see his own unbelief. How many of us in our times of trouble, cannot see beyond our own self-centeredness. We're consumed in our own hurts, fears, insecurities, resentments, bitterness and unforgiveness and yet, we can't even see how they quench God's Spirit.

A dear friend of mine called one day and shared she was battling horrendous negative emotions because her husband of 35 years was planning on divorcing her. She always knew she had years of emotional "walls" that she had built up and never released to God, and she knew that this was probably preventing her from intimately knowing Jesus the way she desired.

She had heard a tape that discussed the importance of making choices by faith to give things over to God and this was why she was calling me. "How do you do this?" she asked. In her heart, she knew this was probably the answer she had so long been waiting for. I concurred and shared, as best I could, the practical application.

Two days later, she called me up and said, "Nan, these principles are absolutely impossible. Ever since I asked God to show me my sin, I've been an absolute emotional basket case! I started two days ago to try to give things over to God, but today I feel I am worse off than when I started. I am consumed with jealousy, bitterness, and anger! I feel like such a failure as a Christian." Now, of course the enemy was right there, whispering all his lies.

I asked her if she had given God permission to expose what He wanted to in her. "Of course, that's the first thing I did," she responded. "Well then," I replied, "Praise Him and thank Him, because He is doing just that! He is showing you your real self! Don't worry, you are right on course. Now, simply recognize what He is bringing up and then go through the steps of giving those things over to Him.

What she forgot was that God must first expose the ungodly thoughts and emotions that are quenching His Spirit, *before* we're able to hand these things over to Him. In other words, *we can't give our sin and self over to Him, if we really don't know what they are!* Because of her ignorance, she was allowing the enemy to, once again, push her into depression.

Scripture never promises that we won't have negative, ungodly and self-centered thoughts, emotions and desires. (Romans 7:15, 19) We're all still human and we'll continue to have these kinds of self-centered soulish thoughts and feelings until we see Jesus. We can have victory over the "desires of our flesh," however, if we constantly make faith choices to give these things over to God, and choose to do what He wants.

Galatians 5:16 tells us that if we choose to "walk after in the Spirit," then we won't carry out the desires of the flesh.

## "At Thy Word, I Will"

Thus, we must *continually* say "not my will, but Thine. Now, again, we might be saying under our breath, "I don't see how You are going to do this. I don't feel like doing it. And, I don't want to do it. But, nevertheless I'm willing to choose to follow You!" What we are really saying is: "I'm willing to do what You ask me to do, simply because I know You love me and I know that You will be faithful to keep Your Promises."

Luke 5:5 is a perfect Scripture here. After Peter spent all night setting his own nets and not catching a thing, Jesus comes along and says to him, "Set your nets." Peter was probably thinking, "I've tried that all night long and it hasn't worked," but nevertheless, he willingly and obediently replies to Jesus: *"At Thy word, I will."*

And, that needs to be our response also. "I don't want to, I don't feel like it, and I don't think it will work; but, nevertheless, "at Thy word, I will!" This response is the only thing that releases the situation into God's hands and the power of the Holy Spirit to come to our aid.

## Endnote:

1. *Times Square Pulpit Series*, David Wilkerson, "Are you mad at God?" 2/16/98.

# Chapter Seven
## *Whose Life Will Be Lived in Your Soul?*

John's wife wanted to divorce him because she was tired of being married and simply wanted out. John did not want the divorce, but his wife proceeded anyway and, amazingly, eventually got custody of their 8-year old daughter, their only child.

Six years went by, and just as John was getting his life back in order, his ex-wife decided to sue him for more child support. She didn't need the money; her motive was simply to destroy him emotionally and financially.

Two days after he was served papers to appear in court, he received a letter from his daughter, who had just turned 14. The letter, he said, was the most horrible, bitter, resentful and unforgiving letter anyone could receive. In that letter he was called *everything*, but human.

At first he was shocked, then angry, then absolutely devastated. He said the only thing that saved him, was knowing how to make faith choices to take his hurts and fears to the Lord, knowing that He would heal them. He said all he could see was "the Cross" and the Scripture that says, "Father, forgive them for they know not what they do." This became his prayer.

After constantly praying and seeking God, John decided to write his daughter a response. Naturally, he wanted to *justify* his own position (his wife was the one who sought the divorce, not him, etc.). But the Lord wouldn't let him do that. Instead, he wrote a four-page letter to his daughter about *how* to take all her hurts to God and *how* to forgive those that have hurt you. He wrote that, "forgiveness is the only thing that will set you free to love."

He asked his daughter's forgiveness for all the things she had named in her letter. He continually re-affirmed his love for her and shared, "even if you want to write things that hurt me, it's okay because I will love you anyway."

A few days later, he received a hand-written post card from his daughter saying, "I don't understand it all or why, but I love you, Daddy, and I do forgive you."

When the court date arrived, both lawyers commented how much the daughter seemed to love her dad. She had evidently held his arm and hugged him the whole time they were in court. The court ruled in John's favor. The ex-wife was so bitter and resentful about the verdict, that John said he had only compassion for her.

John wrote in his letter, "You know what's neat, Nancy, is our being *free* to love. The choice to take the hurts captive and give them to God is ours, but then Jesus gives us the Love we need to respond. In other words, I give Jesus the junk, He then gives me

His Love. What an incredible exchange! Nan, it seems to me so few people understand this..."

## Three Choices

The question that constantly faces us is: "What do we do with the 'justified' negative thoughts and emotions that perpetually bombard us?" Like John, some of us have sufficient grounds (by worldly standards) to be angry, unforgiving and hurt over what has happened and how others have treated us. How do we handle these things?

Well, we have three choices: We can *vent them to others* (which is what many of us have done for most of our Christian lives); we can *stuff them down in the hidden part of our soul* (again, a method many of us have employed in the past); or we can *choose, by faith, to give them to God and be rid of them forever.*

We must understand that we can't hold on to any negative thoughts and feelings without eventually acting out of them. *In other words, undealt-with thoughts and emotions do influence our actions and do control our behavior.* Examples in the Bible of men who didn't deal with their reactions, but simply buried them include: Esau with Jacob; David with Bathsheba; Rueben (and his brothers) with Joseph; and at various instances in the New Testament, with John and Peter.

Even if we try to keep our real thoughts and emotions buried, they still will become the motivation for many of our future actions, whether we're aware of it or not. Burying our hurts, memories, fears—justified or not—does not get rid of them; only allowing God to expose them and giving them over to Him, does.

## Don't Bury Real Feelings

Jesus proclaims in Matthew 16:24 that we are to deny ourselves, pick up our cross and follow Him. As we said earlier, "to deny" in this Scripture does <u>not</u> mean hide, bury, or push down our real thoughts and feelings, even if they are negative, ungodly or evil. As Christians, many of us have been doing this out of ignorance, because we haven't known what else to do with them.

The truth is that God has made us emotional and feeling people and we have <u>no</u> control over what we initially think. Remember, the sin does not occur until after we have chosen to follow, entertain or keep those negative thoughts over what God has prompted us to do. This is the point at which God's Spirit gets quenched and the sin begins.

Therefore, real feelings and thoughts need to be examined, they need to be expressed and they need to be brought forth *before* they lead us to make wrong choices that *will* quench God's Life in us. (James 1:14-15) Our unforgiveness, bitterness and resentment will not go away on their own. They will just continue to accumulate, trigger more negative thoughts and, eventually, produce ungodly actions, unless we allow the Spirit of God to search the hidden part of our soul, expose them and unearth their hold on us.

Thus, it's important we ask God to expose the real *root causes* of our negative thinking so that He can heal us from the inside out. If we simply focus our attention on the *symptoms* that we can see, and not their root causes, those symptoms will return over and over again. Once the root is exposed and dealt with, however, the symptoms will disappear also.

## A Classic Example: Twenty Years of Buried Hurt

The following story is a classic example of the above principles:

Francie wrote to me several years ago after she had attended a retreat where I had spoken. I had given a message on the importance of letting God show us our sin and self (including their root causes), and then dealing with these things as He desires. She told me in her letter that she had such a hard time with these principles, but she wasn't really sure why. Even after she left the retreat, she just couldn't get the study off her mind. Finally, she decided to ask God to expose why she was so upset. "Let's see if this really works," she sarcastically thought to herself. Then she went through the steps of cleansing that I had taught.

God answered Francie's prayer, exposing exactly why she was so upset. He showed her that she still had tremendous resentment and bitterness towards her first husband, who had left her some 20 years before. God showed her that she was reacting to these principles out of those past hurts (she never wanted to think about that man again).

Francie thought she had dealt with all her hurt feelings years ago. In reality, all she had done was bury those negative emotions, and for 20 years she had carried them around with her. After wrestling with God for some time, she decided to go through these steps all over again. Only this time, she wanted to deal with her hurts the proper way. So she asked God to expose her soul.

After sincerely going through the steps of cleansing (that we are about to learn), she said she experienced such a freedom that even her new husband commented that evening, "What's going on! You look so happy!" Even our physical countenance will be changed when we learn to renew our minds and become freed from things we have carried around for years. She sat right down and wrote me a 16-page letter about what the Lord had shown her.

A few weeks later, after I had responded to her, I got another ten-page letter from Francie, telling me of the most exciting miracle of all. Five years previously, she had suffered a major heart attack during an operation. Since then she had been in constant pain and on a heavy dosage of heart medication. When she made the choice to let go of the horrible feelings of hate for her first husband, God supernaturally healed her heart condition. She wrote me that she has had no more pain and has not taken any more heart medication since. The doctor has confirmed her healing and he is totally baffled. I don't believe we realize how closely tied our spiritual and our psychological well-being is with our physical bodies. Healing in one, often, does affect the other.

In order to be truly free of our past and be able to act out of God's Life, we must get rid of our ungodly thoughts and feelings the proper way:  by allowing God to expose them, by looking squarely at them and calling them for what they are, and then by choosing to give these things back over to God and be rid of them forever. (Psalm 103:12)

(If you are interested in further study on how God exposes the root causes of our problems, you might want to get *Be Ye Transformed* and specifically look at Chapters 11-13.)

## Four Steps of Cleansing

What are the steps of cleansing that Francie kept referring to in the above story?  All through the Bible, God tells us to "cleanse our hearts," be an open vessel and give ourselves over to Him, etc.  What do these terms really mean?  How do we do this on a daily and practical level?

My recent, little book called, *The Key* goes into the steps that we are about to learn in much greater detail than I have space for here, and I would really recommend you get it, if the Lord confirms the importance of these steps.  Here, I will only be able to give an overview.

The following "steps" are not something that I have made up or found in some psychology book, they are the actual steps of cleansing and purifying that the priests took in the Temple of Solomon in order to deal with their sin and be reconciled to God.

There are 52 chapters in the Old Testament that deal with the Temple and its importance, thus, I believe, these chapters hold some significance for us also. These cleansing steps are, I believe, God's blueprint or His model or the pattern that He has laid out for us in Scripture in order to deal with our sin and self and be reconciled to Him.

The Scriptural steps for cleansing are: 1) Recognizing and acknowledging our own sin and self; 2) confessing and repenting of all that God shows us and unconditionally forgiving anyone else involved; 3) giving all that God has revealed back to Him; and finally, 4) reading His Word and replacing the lies with His truth. Let's review them in further detail:

## Step One

We are to **recognize and acknowledge the sin and self that has just occurred** in our lives. We are not to vent these thoughts or feelings, nor push them down. We must get alone with God and give them to Him. It's important in this first step to try and describe to the Lord how you are feeling and what you are thinking. Ask Him to expose any "root causes" for your ungodly thoughts, emotions or actions. The more open and honest we can be in expressing how we are really feeling (our humanness), the easier it will be to confess these things to the Lord in the next step. (This is what the priests did at the *Lavers of Bronze* in the Inner Court.)

## Why This Step Is So Important

This first step of recognizing and acknowledging how we feel is critical. Thus, before we go on to Step Two, I would like to expand upon this principle a little further. Remember last chapter, we talked about the importance of seeing our sin *before* we can give it over to the Lord. Well, this is why recognizing and acknowledging the fears, insecurities and doubts that we are experiencing is so important. We need to call them for what they are. Name exactly what we are thinking and feeling. Be truthful; God knows it all anyway. He just wants us to see it for ourselves so we can choose to deal with it.

One woman asked me not too long ago if we should really let out our real feelings out. "Does God want us to do that?" she asked. I told her that God has given us a perfect example in Scripture. Even though David was called "a man after God's own heart," we read how he continually expressed his real thoughts (for example, in Psalm 55:15 and Psalm 109:5-20). If David could express himself in this graphic and explicit way (and God still called him "a man after His own heart"), then we certainly can be honest with God.

Describing and naming what we are feeling is critical, because we can't give something over to God if we really don't know what it is. This is why we must call our feelings for what they are: "I am angry; I am resentful; I feel betrayed; I am fearful." *Experience those thoughts and feelings*. Cry, scream, or yell if you want to. (Remember, we are doing this only to God alone.) This will not only help us understand what we are genuinely feeling, but also it will help us recognize what exactly we are to give over to God.

## An Example: "Give Me Your Real Feelings"

Several years ago, I spent some time with a woman who "in the natural" I didn't really care for. Now, at the time, I couldn't admit the truth to myself, because everyone else absolutely adored her. However, whenever I talked with her, I could feel the phoniness welling up inside me and would always lose my peace.

Finally, I went to the Lord and asked, "Why am I having such a hard time liking this person? Is it me? What's going on? Everyone else loves her." God said to me, "Nancy, you don't like her. Admit it. It's okay. Because," He said, "*I love her. And if you will just give me your real feelings about her, I will give you Mine.*" So, I did just exactly that. I confessed that I really couldn't stand her, but I chose to give those feelings to Him, and He faithfully gave me His Love and His compassion for her (i.e., we "exchanged lives"). The freedom to be "me" returned and I was able to love her with God's Love.

In Psalm 34:4 David declares, "I sought the Lord, and He heard me, and delivered (freed) me from **all** my fears!"

# We're Not To "Relive" The Experiences

One of the reasons acknowledging how we feel is so important, is that we're all human, and we <u>all</u> experience negative, self-centered thoughts and emotions. The freedom comes in when we realize it's okay to feel this way. It's a normal and natural part of being human. *It's how we respond to being aware of our feelings that will determine whether it's sin or not.* In other words, the original negative thought is not sin, it's *what we choose to do with it* that determines if it's sin or not. By recognizing what we are feeling, we'll not only know exactly what to give over to the Lord in the next step, but we'll also be stopping the chain reaction of our soul. Thus, experiencing our emotions is part of dealing with our sin and part of the healing process.

*Now, I <u>don't</u> mean going back and reliving the actual experiences of the past, or visualizing Jesus in the middle of them: I simply mean acknowledging (and, if you have to, crying about) what God has revealed as the root cause that is affecting our choices today.*

Often times I will go through these steps of cleansing, but either because of time pressures or a lack of opportunity, forget to really release my true emotions. A day or so later, I wonder why my peace has not returned. More often than not, it's because I've forgotten to really experience my negative feelings. They are still bottled up within me. Therefore, I must go back and, once again, go through the steps, only this time, acknowledging how I really feel. Again,

*I'm not choosing to follow these emotional feelings, but simply recognizing what they are, so I can give them over to God in the next step.*

## God Takes The "Roots" Away

If God takes the *hidden root causes* of our sin away, we can be assured that the *conscious* negative thoughts and emotions will not occur again over the same issue. In other words, once the hidden part of our soul is emptied and God's Truth put back in, we'll be a cleansed vessel and able to act out of God's Life.

Obviously, we are not accountable for thoughts and feelings that are still hidden and unrevealed to us. However, once God begins to expose these things to us, if we continue at that point to push them back down and not deal with them, it will be sin and it will quench His Spirit. James 4:17 declares, "To him that knoweth to do good (he knows he should make a faith choice and give it over to God), and doeth it not, to him it is sin."

The good news of the Gospel is that, as Christians, we don't have to work at cleaning up our past like psychology teaches, but simply giving God permission to expose the root causes of our present problems. Once He brings up the root, and we are faithful to deal with it as He would have us, then He will remove it "as far as the east is from the west." (Psalm 103:12)

## Step Two

The second step in the cleansing process is that we must: **Confess and repent of everything that the Lord has shown us** in Step One. All that is unholy, unrighteous and "not of faith," we must admit is sin and choose to turn around from following it. *Confession* is simply "acknowledging our sin and self." *Repenting* means to choose to "turn around" from following that sin and self, and choose instead, to follow what God has told us. (Just asking God to forgive us is not enough; we must *first* confess that we have sinned, and then repent of it.)

Recently, I've read some fabulous books about relationships, which eloquently tell us all the things we can do to improve our love and our bond with others, but many of them neglect to share the importance of confession and repentance in that process. Without this, nothing will ever change! Confession and repentance are our own responsibility and the *key* to a changed life. (Again, the priests did this at the *Lavers of Bronze*.)

Psalm 32:5 says, "I acknowledge my sin unto Thee, and mine iniquity have I not hid...I will confess my transgressions unto the Lord; and Thou forgavest the iniquity of my sin."

A part of this important second step is that we must also **unconditionally forgive** anyone else involved in our situation. We have asked God's forgiveness for our sins, now we must unconditionally forgive others of theirs. Unconditional forgiveness simply means releasing that other person into God's hands. It doesn't mean we are pardoning them—that's not our responsibility. We are simply releasing them into God's hands so that *He* can judge them righteously.

Another important point to remember, is that just because we choose to forgive someone, doesn't necessarily mean that we will be able to trust them again, or that we should put ourselves in a similar situation again. God desires that we, by faith, choose to forgive them (or release them to Him) so that He can deal with them appropriately. But this does not mean we trustingly expose ourselves as we did before. Remember Joseph in Genesis 50: He forgave his brothers for trying to kill him, but he never really trusted them again with his life. He forgave them and released them to God, but at the same time, he used *wisdom* in his future dealings with them.

It's interesting to me that nowhere in Scripture does it ever say that we are to trust man; it only tells us we are to trust God. (The one exception to this is Proverbs 31:11 which refers to a husband's trust of his wife's faithfulness.)

## Step Three

The next step of cleansing, is that we must **give over to God all that He has shown us**—not only our specific sin, but also any of our self-centered ways. We are to present our body to God as a "living sacrifice," and then ask Him to continue to expose, cut away and divide the soulish things in our lives from the spiritual. (This step occurs on the *Brazen Altar.*)

"Therefore, I beseech you, my brethren, by the mercies of God, that ye present your bodies a living sacrifice, holy, acceptable unto God, which is your reasonable service." (Romans 12:1-2)

This is the point at which I picture myself on that Brazen Altar in the Inner Court of Solomon's Temple and I pray something like this, "My Jesus, I offer all that I am to You. I choose to willingly surrender *my will* and *my life* to You. May all that pleases You and all that You wish happen."

Now, we can offer Him the sacrifice of praise (Hebrews 13:15), the sacrifice of righteousness (Psalm 4:5) and the sacrifice of thanksgiving (Psalm 116:17; 107:22). These are called 'sacrifices' because, much of the time, we really don't "feel" like praising God, or being thankful or being joyful, but we do it anyway *by faith*.

## Step Four

Finally, we must **read God's Word and replace the lies with the Truth**. In step Three, we sacrificed to God all the things He showed us that quenched His Spirit. It's important to replace those things with His Word and His Love. The priests of Solomon's Temple actually bodily got up into the *Molten Sea* (a huge bathtub holding 2000 baths) in order to cleanse themselves. And it's the same thing with us.

As we read His Word, He promises to cleanse and heal our souls with the "washing of the water of the Word." (Ephesians 5:26) It's only God's Word that can totally restore us at this point. Only God can wash us in His Love and heal us with His Word. Some great Scriptures to read here are: 1 John 1:5-10; Psalm 51; 32:1-5 and 2 Corinthians 7:1.

At this point, whether we feel like it or not, we have been cleansed, renewed and filled with God's Life so we can now boldly walk into the Holy Place just like the priests did, *worship the Lord at the Incense Altar* and petition our prayers. (1 Chronicles 16:29; Hebrews 10:19, 22)

## Worshiping the Lord

Remember, until we are clean, God told us that He would not hear us, nor would we be able to hear Him. (Isaiah 59:2) Coming into the Lord's presence, communing with Him and being one in the Spirit are what worshiping is all about.

George Barna, the president of a marketing research company in California, says that most Christians would acknowledge their responsibility to worship the Lord, but admit that they rarely connect with Him. I believe it, again, goes back to our not knowing how to make faith choices. If we don't know we have God's authority to make choices we don't feel, like Francie in the above story, we won't know how to "cleanse ourselves." And if we don't know how to become a cleansed vessel, we won't be able to come into God's presence and worship Him.

Worship means *to kiss, to prostrate oneself* (or touch one's nose to the ground). It means to bow down or to show absolute submission. But the definition of worship that I really like, is that worship means *"to catch fire."* I love that, because I can almost visualize catching fire with the Love of God! Worshiping God is different than simply praising Him. Praising God is what the priests of Solomon's Temple did when they *first* entered the Outer Courts of the Temple. And this is *the first thing* we are to do when we begin our prayer time to seek the Lord. Scripture tells us that God "inhabits our praises" (Psalm 22:3), and this is exactly what we are imploring (or asking) Him to do in us.

Worshiping the Lord, however, is something totally different. Worshiping God is what the temple priests did *last*. They worshiped God *after* they were cleansed, *after* they brought their incense offerings to the Golden Altar, after they took off their shoes, and *after* they prostrated themselves before the Golden Altar.

In other words, there's a proper procedure to follow in order to enter God's presence, be able to worship Him and ask our petitions. Listen to Psalm 24:3-4, which tells us what must happen first: "Who shall ascend into the hill of the Lord? Or who shall stand in His Holy Place? [Only] *He who hath clean hands (or soul) and a pure heart (or spirit)..."* (See Psalm 32:6.)

Once the priests came into the Holy Place, they sprinkled incense over the hot coals, fell on their faces and worshiped the Lord. (Leviticus 16:12-13) In like manner, this is the point where we enter God's presence, place our love offerings on the altar and fall on our face to worship Him in "spirit and truth," and He promises to meet with us. (John 4:23-24; Exodus 30:6, 36) *We're not asking Him for anything, but simply there to adore, revere and love Him.*

## Praying our Petitions

After we worship him, we can pray our petitions "in His Name" and He promises to hear us, because we are, at that moment, truly one with Him in the Spirit. (John 16:24) In other words, He will act upon our prayers, not simply because we have attached "in His Name;" *we are literally joined and united "in His Name" while we are praying them.*

When our prayer time is over, just like the priests, we can go out and share of the fullness of the Lord that we have received while worshiping Him at the altar of our hearts where He met with us.

This is what Francie did and why her husband remarked on how different she looked. For those moments, because she had been *in the Lord's presence*, she was reflecting His image. Remember in Exodus, where Moses saw the Lord face to face and because of that encounter, was radically and physically changed. In fact, so much so, that he had to wear a veil to cover his face. (Look up Exodus 34:33-34)

I'm so excited about some of the *new* things that I have recently learned about the importance of learning to worship the Lord, not just on Sundays, but daily in our own prayer closets. For example, did you know that there is a direct correlation between worshiping the Lord and having the joy of our salvation *restored*? This gift of joy comes only as a result of being before His presence in worship. (Psalm 16:11)    I shared some of the things I am learning about worship with audiences in Australia and New Zealand this past month, and they were ecstatic. They said they couldn't wait to go home and put into practice some of the things they heard. Thus, I feel strongly that the Lord wants my next little *Plain and Simple* book to be on "worship" and to be entitled, *Private Worship: The Key to Joy.*

## Yielded To The Holy Spirit

In summary, I pray that the Holy Spirit will continually remind us of the importance of setting aside our own natural, emotional way of thinking (by going through the above four steps of cleansing) and choosing to follow the Lord in whatever He tells us to do. If we can learn to do this, then, as Romans 12:2 promises, we will be *transformed into His Image* and able to experience, not only His abundant Life, but also intimacy with Him. (2 Corinthians 3:18)

Transformation is God's goal for each of us. He wants us to live the Truth, where our words and our deeds match, so that the Gospel can be passed on. The real key to our being able to do this, however, is our *own* willingness to follow Him *regardless* of how we feel, what we think or what we desire. Staying an open and cleansed vessel so that God's Life can flow through us (being single-minded) is the secret to the victorious Christian life.

2 Corinthians 12:9 tells us that, "...My grace is sufficient for thee; for My strength is made perfect in weakness. Most gladly therefore, will I rather glory in my infirmities, so that the power of Christ may rest upon me."

This is simply saying that God's divine strength can exist in us only when we are open and yielded vessels. Now, *weakness* in the above Scripture does not mean feebleness or inability, but rather a person who is totally yielded and surrendered to God. Paul uses this word *weakness* in 2 Corinthians 13:4 when he explains, "...Jesus was crucified through weakness." Certainly, Jesus was not a weak person, but a totally yielded Son whom God could use in whatever way He desired. This "yieldedness" is God's plan for us also.

Yieldedness is not an attitude of "I give up" or "I don't care anymore." This response is really a self-centered defense mechanism and a way of protecting oneself from further hurts. This is not the attitude that God is speaking about here.

The Christian yieldedness that God is referring to, is a kind of neutral gear—a type of surrendering, yielding or relinquishing everything, so that we are cleansed, ready, willing and waiting to do whatever God asks, whenever He wants. It's simply *willing obedience* where we say, "Lord, I'm ready, cleansed and willing; use me in any way You want."

## Be a Hosea

Hosea in the Old Testament is a wonderful example of one who willingly surrendered himself to do God's will. In other words, he loved God so much that he willingly laid down his life so that God could reach his adulterous wife, Gomer, through him.

In his own power and strength, Hosea could never have loved Gomer the way he did. Yet, because of his faithfulness to love God first, choosing to yield his will and life totally to Him, God enabled him to become the instrument by which He reached Gomer.

Jesus is also our example. He is the Creator of the universe and yet, He chose of His own free will to lay His Life down for us. He was the mediator, the channel and the vessel of God's Love to us. He died so that God's Love could be released through Him to us. "Hereby perceive we the Love of God, because He laid down His life for us: and *we ought to [choose to] lay down our lives for the brethren.*" (1 John 3:16)

The question is: "Are you willing to do the same? *Are you willing to be a Hosea*? Are you willing to, moment by moment, allow God to use your life to reach others?"

These are questions each of us will face a hundred times a day, everyday, for the rest of our lives as Christians.

The inward life of the Spirit can only be gained by a passionate and consuming love for God. How much do you love Him enough to surrender *everything* to Him? The walk of faith necessary for experiencing His presence and His fullness is not easy.

As Matthew 7:14 tells us, "Straight is the gate, and narrow is the way, *which leads to life*, and [only] a few there be that [will] find it."

The reason only a few find that abundant Life and that intimacy with Christ, is because the way to get there goes **against the tide**.

How about you?  Do you love God enough to *choose* to go through that narrow gate and down that hard path?

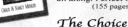

 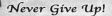

The King's HIGH Way

# UNDERSTANDING GOD'S TRUTH

In this sequel to *The Way of Agape*, Chuck and Nancy teach us the practical application of renewing our minds. Only in *putting off* our fears, anxieties, depression, anger, and unbelief and *putting on* Christ can we be free to reflect Him in all we do. Outlines at the back of each chapter contain all the Scriptural references.

### Additional Resources:

Textbook
Personal Application Workbook
DVD Series (7 Sessions)
DVD Bible Study Package
Leader's Guide
CD Audio
MP3 Audio

## 1-866-775-KING

On the Internet:
http://www.kingshighway.org